Paper Garden

and Other Stories

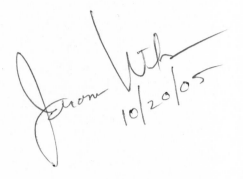

Jerome Wilson

10/20/05

Paper Garden

and Other Stories

By

Jerome Wilson

This book contains works of fiction. All characters and events portrayed are fictitious or are used fictitiously.

Paper Garden and Other Stories

Kerlak Enterprises, Inc., Memphis, TN 38115
Copyright © 2005 Jerome Wilson
Cover Photgraphs by Adam Remsen
ISBN-13:978-0966074-48-2
ISBN-10: 0-966-0744-8-3
Library of Congress Cataloging-in-Publication Data
Library of Congress Control Number: 2005924752

Kerlak Enterprises, Inc.
Publication Division
www.kerlak.com
This book is printed on acid-free paper.
Printed in the United States of America

Contents

INTRODUCTION

Farm-raised Catfish and Cellular Phones: Jerome Wilson and the New Music of the Mississippi Delta

Born In The Camp With Six Toes cut me with a knife
Baby Gauge sucked the poison out
Oh Sweet Jesus the levees that break in my heart.
— Frank Stanford, "The Snake Doctors"
[*From The Light the Dead See: Selected Poems of Frank Stanford*, ed. Leon Stokesbury. Fayetteville, Arkansas: University of Arkansas Press, 1991. 36.]

I remember the first time I had dinner with Jerome Wilson (sometimes, most of the time, we call him Willie J., for that is his name). For some reason, I had a hankering for sushi. Willie J. paused for a moment, gave not a frown but a look of bemusement, and said, "Okay." It was not until we were seated at the restaurant — directly across the street from the historic Peabody Hotel in Memphis – that he informed me raw fish had never once crossed his lips. A little embarrassed, remembering how some newbies to sushi can be horrified by the notion, more true of Southerners than with most, I offered that we leave immediately and mosey over to the Rendezvous, whose dry ribs are always a welcome delight. But no, he said, he was looking forward to this sushi-thing; he wanted to try. And try he did. With much gusto I might add. He really dug wasabi. In fact, within the next year Willie J. was frequently inviting me to come to dinner with him and friends — over sushi. Soon eating sushi in Memphis became synonymous in my mind with the brilliant young writer, Jerome Wilson.

That twist, that seeming incongruity, that acquiescence to the present, to the here-and-now truth of the world, is what makes Wilson's fiction so galvanizing. Or, to be more precise, one of the many elements that makes them so delicious. Wilson writes out of a grand tradition of Southern writers, and of black writers, but also of the iconoclasts and outsiders and grotesques and dreamers that are the sand in the mouth of the great oyster that creates the pearl we think of as American literature.

"Paper Garden" reminds me more than anything

of the work of the late poet, Frank Stanford (1948-1978), who grew up on the banks of the Mississippi and wrote extensively about his childhood there and of the electric collision among European, African, and Native culture. His poetry is quintessentially American due to that wonderful and frank recognition. His only agenda is to tell it like it is, to tell it right, and to tell it good.

So, too, Jerome Wilson tells it in stories like "Paper Garden" and "The Witness Tree" and so many others in this collection. His vision updates those old hants of the South with new chains and new insights. His multi-variant prose is pungent, not simply folksy, rather he knows how to exploit the vernacular to dazzling effect, much like his spiritual forefather, the great short-story writer James Allan McPherson.

("The first thing we do is get Mama's turkey leg. She munching and pointing and saying how good her turkey is. She lean down and give me a bite. It is good and I ask for another. Then another, until finally Mama said: 'Look, Sonny Buck.' Which is the same as saying, 'Now, you ain't gonna eat all of my leg!'" – "A Trip to the Fair.")

The apparent intimacy of these stories belies their knowledge of the wide world – of politics and race relations and religion. But always these narratives return to the subject of family and relationships and the mythopoetic palpability of the land. Like my favorite of the bunch, "The Croquet Players," in which a group of ne'er-do-wells get slowly soused while picnicking and playing croquet down by the river whereupon they discover a dead body, and continue drinking and playing while deciding whether or not they should call the police.

("Finally, Fi-Fi decides that she had enough of this. 'What is big deal here? I will call police. You Americans are insane totally.' She is throwing up her hands, spilling her martini down her back, and grabbing another one from her daughter with the other hand. 'I do not understand.'")

More often than not these stories are set in Memphis, or in the landscape that surrounds that Delta metropolis, so close to its agrarian past/present, its race-thick obsessions, its Mississippi River Culture and peculiarities and Protestant weirdness. (In Memphis anything east of the intersection of Poplar and Highland is called "East Jesus, Tennessee.")

These stories are as current as 50 Cent and as old as tales of Middle Passage, slavery, and sharecropping. The American Delta's past is the ur-American past; it contains the strangeness, the facts, the blood, the hate, the humanity, and the ingenuity that makes the United States possible. Many Americans, a large quantity of them living in Memphis, want to capture and freeze Memphis in its Yellow Fever past, to make it all about Elvis and cotton, the assassination of Dr. Martin Luther King, Jr. and W.C. Handy. But Jerome Wilson is not playing that game. His fiction acknowledges Vietnamese restaurants and too-much traffic, head-bangers, rave parties and the Third Iteration of the Reverend Al Green. Yet he doesn't forget the roots of neighborhood and Southern mores (both among black folks and white folks) that kept Tennesseeans from slitting each other's collective throats and that has allowed them to thrive and move forward into the 21st century.

Yes, there is much news in these stories, but there is art and heart and – that ole Memphis standby – soul. If Willie J. Wilson wrote and played music, I'm sure he'd do the ghosts of Stax Records proud.

These stories bear witness and sing a powerful song.

Randall Kenan

Author's Note

"I imagined myself traveling from town to town, city to city, looking for a Miss Marion. Stories would spring up about me, about some kid looking for a friend that he met one summer. Toothless old men with guitars will be moaning some sad song about lost friendship and loneliness and how cruel the world can get without a good friend or a faithful dog. I will become a legend. Of course, some folks will say I never existed, but just somebody's crazy imagination gone wild. But that wouldn't get me down, since worrying about that kind of stuff doesn't bother me none anyway."

— "Paper Garden," Jerome Wilson

PAPER GARDEN

Back in the days when life was easy and you could walk down the street at night and not worry about anybody knocking you over the head with some blunt object and taking all of your pocket change, Miss Mamie Jamison, the neighborhood kids' godmother who gave us money and candy and let us hide in her parlor when the big boys chased us from the playground, took seriously ill one summer and had to be put to bed. Her daughter, the one all the way from New York, moved in with her, often dressed in nothing but what looked like black body suits and tall fruit-basket hats like that Chiquita woman wears on banana peels. If it wasn't black body suits, she was wearing a pair of men's trousers and shirt along with a mighty fine pair of work boots. But despite her icky clothes, she looked like a movie star from the silent screens: deep, dark black hair, thin red lips, and that pale powdery skin color, like she was waiting for some invisible director to yell "action!" and give her the go-ahead to say her lines like that was the only thing God created her for.

Of course, the only reason the Chiquita woman, Miss Marion, wasn't talked about like a dog too much by the other ladies in the neighborhood was because she was from New York. Meaning Miss Marion obviously knew what the latest fashions were and knew much more about fads and styles than these country women, including my own mama, would ever know in their whole life-time. This was also why she was called "Miss" Marion even by the old folks—the way she spoke, calling everybody "darling" and "sweetie" and always saying how much she loves somebody, even complete strangers she met walking down the street. You would have thought they were blood relatives.

My mama was the main gofer over Miss Marion and would come home just about every other day with some catchy word or phrase that she had heard Miss Marion say, or what someone else had heard her say. Once, while leaving out the door to go to a Daughters of the Confederate Army meeting, Mama said to Papa and me, "I'll be back in about an hour. Chow." When she closed the door, Papa, with a puzzled look on his face, looked up from his evening paper and asked me, "What dog?"

Something was happening to the town of Harper.

All the women wanted to be Miss Marion, ordering just about every dress and hat and scarf and shoe that the Sears Roebuck catalog had to offer. Even the men, down to the youngest and up to the oldest, watched Miss Marion out of the corner of their eyes. We watched how she switched her way through town knowing full well everybody was looking at her in a skirt that was at least ten inches too short and ten years ahead of Harper's time. Eddie T. sat on that old tree stump at the end of the main street playing his harmonica. Though he claimed that he was blind, he wrote and sang a song about her that teetered on the edge of vulgarity, sometimes drawing a good crowd and a nice pile of spending money in his ragged hat that he kept between his feet, if it was a Saturday.

Even Papa, whenever he saw Miss Marion coming up on our side of the sidewalk, all of a sudden had to go check the oil in the car, or he had to go clip the hedges, or the grass was too tall and he had to go cut it. I think Mama knew what Papa was up to, but it was a summer and it was hot and the price of ground beef had dropped and life was just too wonderful so Mama didn't say anything. "At least he's away from that paper," she said. It was true: Papa had about three weeks worth of *Harper's Sentinel*'s piled up on the coffee table. Most times now, he spent looking out the big picture window.

It wasn't long before Miss Marion had announced that she would start giving acting lessons down at the community center, since she had some acting degree from NYU and saw that it was not only a good deed but "an absolute duty"—another one of her catchy phrases that she almost wore out—that she bring some of her "expertise" back home to those who weren't as fortunate as herself.

So, to be honest, I wasn't the least bit surprised when I came home from playing kickball with Terry and Kicky when Mama asked me if I were planning to take any acting lessons from Miss Marion—as if we had already discussed it before.

"I thought you were going to play football this summer, Sonny Buck?" Papa asked me, not even giving my head the chance to let the first question sink in good.

"And what's wrong with acting lessons?" Mama asked Papa in that tone of voice that said you best watch what you say.

Papa caught the hint, so he shuffled around in his favorite chair, the one that sits in front of the television set, then he lowered his newspaper just enough so we could see his eyes. "There's nothing wrong with taking acting lessons if that's what Sonny Buck wants to do. I just thought maybe he wanted to play football since he's been playing for the last three summers."

"Well, missing football this year is not going to kill him none. I think it will do you some good to expand your culture, Sonny Buck. I'll give you ten dollars." Then she gave Papa that look that told him that he had better not bid against her. And when he didn't, she said, "Good. Now that's settled. The class starts Monday."

I looked over at Papa, but he was already behind his paper again. So there I was.

But it wasn't bad. Come to find out, all the mothers in the neighborhood—except for Kicky's mama—made their kids go see Miss Marion for acting lessons, which consisted mainly of remembering some line from a Shakespeare play and reciting it while she shouted how you should be standing, or lecturing you on the proper facial expression, or having fits on when you should be breathing. And if you weren't doing it just right, she would just get all undone: flapping her arms, twisting her face, then sometimes dropping to her knees and saying, "Lord, please help me educate these ignorant people." That ignorant part was something we didn't feature too well and Debra Ann told her so, being since Debra Ann was brought up that way; that is, brought up to cuss grown folks out and not think twice about it.

But Miss Marion took an interest in me. She didn't yell when I read, but watched me with her mouth hanging open, telling everybody to knock off the noise back there—mainly Kicky and Terry and another boy we called Scootie, who could make funny noises with his armpits. Miss Marion said that I was talented.

What'd she say that for? I recited Shakespeare for Mama and Papa almost every evening before, during and after dinner. Papa said that I was real good. Mama said I was a born actor. A genius was the word Miss Robbins—the school's English teacher who doubled as the drama coach in the springtime—used one night when she came over just to hear me read a few lines from *A Midnight Summer's Dream*. I was good. No lie. I imagined myself going to Hollywood, or to New York like Miss Marion, and becoming a real actor like James Cagney or Humphrey Bogart and star in films where I get to shoot the bad guy and run off with his dame because he's nothing but a big gorilla and she had been giving me the eye all along at the bar between sippings of tequilas and straight shots of brandy. I was Othello hanging upside down from the big tree in our front yard; I was Romeo on the football field. At the groceries: Puck. At the gas station with Papa: Macbeth. Then Henry VIII, then Hamlet, then King Lear and I couldn't stop. Terry and Kicky couldn't keep up and came close to hating me, something I couldn't blame them for. For I was crazy. I figured if I didn't make it in pro football, at least I had my acting talents to fall back on.

But the jist of this story really didn't kick in until about a month later, a July evening; Terry and Kicky were over my house for dinner: Terry was fat and would eat anything that couldn't get up and run, but Mama always invited Kicky over because she said Kicky was from a dysfunctioning family on account of his daddy been to jail about ten times and his mama was always hooking up with somebody who was going to Memphis for a couple of days. So, sometimes, if Kicky didn't eat with us, he didn't eat.

"So, how's the acting coming along?" Papa asked Terry and me.

Terry, between mouthfuls of some hot meatball dish—a recipe Mama got from Miss Marion – said, "It's okay. We studying *Romeo and Juliet*. Can I have some water?"

"Oh, that's nice," Mama said. "I remember in the springtime the senior class would always put on *Romeo and Juliet* out on the front lawn of the school. That's how we paid for the prom every year. I was Juliet. We decorated the whole stage with honeysuckles and white clovers and I wore a crown of white roses." Mama smiled. "I was beautiful then."

Papa said, "What do you mean? You're still beautiful."

Mama looked up at Papa, just like everybody else at the table did. I remember one time he was telling everybody down at the lodge how his boy was going to make the football team and go on to play for some Ivy League school. But I remember getting cut the first week of tryouts, so I hid out over Kicky's house all day long. It didn't do any good; Papa knew exactly where I was because Debra Ann told him out of spite on account of me not wanting to carry her books after school. When he found me, he said, "Let's go home, Sonny Buck," and the way he said it I knew I had let him down. At home Papa got on the phone and called an emergency meeting being since he was sort of like the vice-president of the lodge. He told me to come with him. When we got there all the men were fussing and wondering what was so important. Then Papa said, "This is my son,

William 'Sonny Buck' Jackson and he didn't make the little league football team. If he never makes any other team in his life, he's still my boy and I love him. And if any of you say anything out of pocket, I'll bust your damn noses." Then we went down to Olive Branch and he bought me a beer at Tang's. Papa said not to say anything about the nose busting or the beer drinking being since he was sort of like a deacon at church. That was the only time I ever remember Papa saying or doing something profound and not being behind his paper.

At the table Mama put her napkin up to her face and dabbed at the corner of her eyes. "Frank, you're so kind. I love you. I love you all." Then she got up and went around the table kissing everybody. Just like Miss Marion, except Mama wasn't performing. Even Kicky probably wanted to cry; I don't think he had ever been kissed by his mother.

And right then and there I made a vow that if ever the moon and the sun and all the constellations ever decided to twist, switch up, collide or explode in the heavens and cause me to lose my mind and want to run away from home, I was going to take these two beloved people with me.

After dinner, Mama told me to take a plate of rum muffins over to Miss Marion. She told Kicky and Terry to go with me, but they suddenly claimed to hear their mothers calling them. So I had to go by myself. I picked up the plate and said "Chow" to everybody.

When I got to house, I was standing in an open doorway. "Miss Marion?" I peeped in, looking into a dark living room full of bulky antique furniture, the stench of Vick's vapor rub and the confined wet musty smell like after a long hot summer rain creeping out on the porch with me and tingling my nose. "Miss Marion?" I repeated.

"William, is that you?"

I peeped farther into the room and saw a figure move in a chair over in a corner. "Yes, this is me."

"Well, why you out there? Come in here."

I walked in, bumped into something, and she clicked on a table lamp.

She had been drinking. She wasn't wearing a hat. Her hair was down and she was more white than usual except for her eyes: bloodshot and veiny red-like.

"You okay, Miss Marion?"

"I couldn't be better," she said slowly, and then she brought a glass up to her mouth and sipped.

I stood there watching, not knowing what to do, but then I remembered why I had come. "My mama sent you these." I held the plate out in front of me. "She made rum muffins."

She laughed. "That's all I need." She downed the rest of her drink. Then she frowned up at me like I was something awful. "Do you know how evil the world is?"

"Excuse me?" I asked, steady holding onto the plate of muffins because I was too nervous to do anything else.

"The world is full of evil. You knew that, didn't you?"

"Ahh...yes, I knew that."

"But you know, I don't think anybody else knows about this world but me and you." She burped. "I don't think most folks know they're mean. If they don't know any better, how do you expect them to act good? You see what I'm saying, William?"

"Yes, I think so."

"You know what bad thing I did one time? I made this fat girl cry. When I was up in New York I went to this restaurant with this friend of mine and he brought his girlfriend with him. She was as big as a house. I don't know what Judd saw in her. She must've pissed Jack Daniels. I don't know. Anyway, I think I was drinking, I can't remember, but I remember telling this girl that I bet she eats a lot. Then Judd tells me that she's a vegetarian. A vegetarian. Can you believe that, William? A three hundred pound vegetarian?"

I shook my head no.

"I couldn't believe it either. So I ask him what in the hell has his vegetarian been snacking on? A damn California redwood? I thought it was funny, but she started crying and Judd was trying to hush her up because everybody was looking at us. The more she cried the louder I got until they put all of us out of the restaurant. They didn't have good food anyway. But now I feel so bad about what I said. I got to tell everybody what I've done. That's my punishment." She grabbed some tissue from a roll of toilet paper and dabbed at her eyes and blew her nose. "You know, I think this world would be lot better place to live if everyone would just do as I say. Know what I'm talking about, William?"

"Miss Marion," I hesitated, "are you drunk?"

"Not yet, but I have the potential of becoming an outstanding alcoholic. You just give me time."

I didn't say a word. I picked up the roll of toilet paper and tore some off, and out of nervousness started playing with it as Miss Marion was steady talking—mainly about how much money her mama had spent on her education and now she can't even find an acting job off Broadway. I twisted the paper—tucking it here, pulling it there, twisting the bottom—until finally, I had created a little flower, something between a carnation or a rose, but a nice looking flower just the same. We both looked down at the object in my hand; I think I was more surprised.

She took the flower from me and started crying. "You know what this is, William?"

"A paper flower?"

"No," between sobs, "this is beauty. Painful beauty. You're just like me. You can look right through pain and see the beauty of it. This is painful beauty. Thank you, William."

I was ready to go home. I tried to throw a hint by moving closer to the door and shuffling my feet like I suddenly heard someone calling my name.

"Sit down, William," she said, "and make me some more," handing me the roll of paper. She refilled her glass, then leaned back on the couch. "You got it, William."

"Got what, Miss Marion?" I asked, steady making the paper flowers.

"It! You got that third eye right here— "she tapped her forehead—"and you can see right down that narrow line. I can't see that line as clearly as I want to. I never seen anybody read Shakesphere like you can. How do you do it? You ain't got to answer that. Most folks who are good at something usually don't know how they do it."

Since it wasn't a big roll, I had quickly made about twenty flowers and they were on the floor around my feet.

Miss Marion dropped to her knees and ran her fingers through the flowers like they were gold coins. "These are beautiful." Then, like a sudden after-thought: "I'll be back. I got to go check on mama."

She disappeared down the dark hallway, leaving me alone in the parlor. I was trying to decide whether to leave, figuring that she was too drunk to remember whether I was here or not, but that wouldn't be a proper thing to do. By the time I had made up my mind to make a break for the door, Miss Marion came back with a flashlight and two new rolls of toilet paper.

"Mama's doing just fine. Let's go."

"Where we going?"

Miss Marion looked at me like I had a hole in my head. "Outside. We're going to plant these beautiful flowers in the garden. You don't actually think that I'm going to let all of these flowers just multiply inside my house, do you?"

Though it was late, about eight or nine, it was still hot. Miss Marion started digging small holes in the empty garden with her fingers. She placed a flower in the hole and then she mashed the soft dirt around the paper stem. She was quiet, working quickly, stopping every once in a while to take a sip from the bottle that she had brought out here, or to grab some more paper flowers from me, or to tell me where to shine the flashlight. This went on for about an hour until we had the whole flowerbed in the front yard covered in paper flowers.

Miss Marion started crying again. "This is just damn lovely!"

We stood there in the night looking at the paper garden. It really did look nice.

"You know, William, some things are just too good for this world." Then she looked up at me like she was expecting me to add to what she had just said. But I kept my eyes on the garden.

Fortunately, I heard Papa calling me and I told Miss Marion that I had to go. I started running down the street, pushing what she had said off to the side somewhere.

She yelled, "Good-bye, William. Come back in the morning and we can see how beautiful this garden looks in the daylight!"

"Okay," I yelled, running wildly in the middle of the street like I had just been set free out of a cage, looking back only once just in time to see her wave at me and take another sip.

But the next day it rained, a thunderstorm so terrible that even Mama said, "Maybe you shouldn't go to class today, Sonny Buck. Miss Marion will understand." I sat in the house all day until the rain stopped around early evening.

Later I walked down to Miss Marion's house and stood in front of the paper garden. The rain had melted the flowers and the only thing that was left was soggy toilet paper all over the yard. I stared at the garden for a long time.

I knocked on the door, but there wasn't an answer. I peeped through the windows into the parlor but I didn't see anything. Once, I thought I saw Miss Marion ducking down the dark hallway, but I wasn't sure. I knocked on the door and yelled her name, but there was no answer. I went home.

Suddenly, everything changed. Not a change back, not a change forward, but a change like the closing scene of a play when the curtain comes down and you wonder were you really there. Like the melting of the paper garden was an omen of what was to happen next, Miss Mamie Jamison died toward the end of the summer. She was buried the next day, then the next day after that Miss Marion packed up everything in the middle of the night and left, and not too long after that the house was boarded up. Just like that. Then slowly Harper went back to the way it was: boring. Like a rubber band, Harper had stretched to accommodate one of its own, then quickly snapped back into place—nothing different, but the same. My mother went back to her meatloaf on Mondays, spaghetti on Tuesdays, and pork chops, chicken, roast, noodles and stew on the other days. I went back to my football practices and Papa slipped back behind his paper.

Once, I wondered if Miss Marion was a real person, or if she was one of those fallen angels who comes to earth to earn her wings. You would wonder about anybody who steps into a person's life and charms and dazzles you, forces your imagination to soar higher than the heavens, then for no reason, quietly disappears, never realizing that someone has been left behind whose love for life is now running on an uncontrollable high. Though it didn't last long, for one brief moment in my life, I wasn't William "Sonny Buck" Jackson, the junior varsity football player. Instead, I was William "Sonny Buck"

Jackson, the Broadway star, the Hollywood actor—the whole town not the town, but a stage; the townspeople not the townspeople, but the audience. Maybe Miss Marion knew what she was doing and was just giving me a taste of what could be, letting me know that there's a different world outside the four walls of Harper.

I wondered what had become of Miss Marion. I imagined myself traveling from town to town, city to city, looking for a Miss Marion. Stories would spring up about me, about some kid looking for a friend that he met one summer. Toothless old men with guitars will be moaning some sad song about lost friendship and loneliness and how cruel the world can get without a good friend or a faithful dog. I will become a legend. Of course, some folks will say I never existed, but just somebody's crazy imagination gone wild. But that wouldn't get me down, since worrying about that kind of stuff doesn't bother me none anyway.

Sweet Jessie Leigh

We all sitting out on the porch. We—being me, Thomas and Big Ma—just watching the sun go down over there at the edge of Mr. L.C.'s cotton fields. Dudley gets to barking and not too long before we see somebody coming up the road. None of us can see too good since it's getting close to dark.

"Now who is that?" That was Big Ma.

We all squinting and carrying on. Thomas—he starts pointing cause he's stone deaf and he don't know we already looking at whoever that is coming up the road. So he's steady pointing.

The figure is some kind of strange. First, it looks like some old woman with bundles on her back. But then, as she gets closer, she shaping into a old man, limping, cause of the heavy bundle. We can't see his face, since he's still some distance away and it's close to dark.

Thomas pointing and hopping around on the porch. Big Ma points to a chair and signals for him to sit down. He does, but he's still too excited, so he's just twisting in his seat.

I'm standing on the steps behind Big Ma who's standing all out in the yard, hands on her hips and just going to town on looking. And Dudley just ripping the wind with his barking. "Shut up, dog!" That's Big Ma.

Slowly, the old man comes. It ain't long 'til he's almost at the edge of the yard and then suddenly, all of us back at the house find out that this ain't no old man at all. He's a white boy. Not too much older than me, being about sixteen or seventeen and no more. He's up in the yard, coming toward us, carrying a bundle of some kind, sweaty dusty face, dirty clothes and all.

"Can I help you?" ask Big Ma soon as the boy step into hearing distance.

"Yes, ma'am," he say, standing in the middle of the yard, not too far from Big Ma. "Can you spare me a cup of water?" He drop his stuff on the ground and suddenly he's taller.

Big Ma, not turning around to look at me, but still looking at him: "Jessie Leigh, go bring this fellow some water from the barrel."

But I still stand there, next to Thomas, watching him cause he's some sight with his motley looking self.

"Don't stand there gaping, gal! Run on!"

I run around the house, looking for an empty can around the yard. I rinse it out real good before I fill it up with water from the barrel. I hear them talking, Big Ma asking him where he from and he telling her he's from some funny named place up North. I come back to the front.

"You look mighty young. What you doing down here?"

I step out and give Big Ma the can. She gives it to him and he takes it, almost grabbing it, and starts drinking—gulping it down like he never had none before.

Finally: "Looking for work," he say.

"Oh."

Dudley, he's all around the stranger, sniffling and carrying on. He gets too close to the bundle and the boy say, "Get away, dog!" Dudley growl and walk on off.

For the first time, he notice me and Thomas. Big Ma—she see him staring at us. "This my grand-daughter, Jessie Leigh," darting her head back in my direction and I stick my finger in my mouth and bow my head cause I can feel him looking at me and I'm shame. "And that's my grand boy," darting her head over at Thomas who's out in the yard catching lightning bugs. "My boy's children. Couldn't take care of them so I took them. The boy's stone deaf. She ain't too right herself."

I'm shame, so I run in the house and peep through the curtains.

He's through with the can, throwing the few drops on the ground, handing the can to her. "Thank you, ma'am."

"You mighty welcome." She drop the can right there in the yard.

He picks up his bundle, slinging it over his back and walks off. Me and Big Ma watch him go. Thomas steady running around not caring about too much of nothing. The boy way down the road now, just a tiny speck.

The first thing I hear when Big Ma come inside the house: "That trash had another thing coming if he figured on staying here! That's why I came out into the yard, met him before he could hit the porch cause I wasn't letting him come another further! The trash!"

I go to my room and bury my head in my pillow so I don't have to hear her fuss. It ain't a wind nowhere; like me, it's tired, too. As I lie on my pallet, the moon come out, shining over the tall trees. The light is coming through the holes in my curtains. Big

Ma through fussing now, and I'm falling asleep.

"Jessie Leigh! Jessie Leigh! Wake yourself up, gal!"

I wake up and the room is just full of sun. I'm rubbing my eyes, yawning and stretching. I start to lie back down but Big Ma holler again.

"Jessie Leigh!"

I get up, put some clothes on. I go to the kitchen and I see Thomas already at the table jabbing oatmeal in his mouth.

"Hurry up and get you something to eat," Big Ma say. She's sitting over there in a corner peeling peaches, letting the hulls drop over in this big bucket that she got sitting between her legs.

Thomas a greedy thing. He ate up most of the oatmeal, so I get me two pieces of bacon, a biscuit and make me a sandwich. He humming to hisself, licking the bowl and smiling at me cause he know I can't have none. I roll my eyes and swallow.

Big Ma stops peeling, sitting the bucket down in her seat. She picks up her bags that's sitting by the table. "Lord, my back," she say. "I'm fixing to go." Before she leave, she get her hat that's hanging over there by the door and put it on her head.

She walking out through the yard. I watch her. She's a skinny old woman, tall and light-skinned, long good hair.

I ain't too sure, but she might not like me. She told me not to go back to school no more, since she need me working around the house and all that learning won't do no kind of good if we're starving. We not go to church either, since she said if the Lord be Lord then why are we poor, why is Thomas stone deaf, and why come I ain't got good sense. That's what she told me and that's she told Amy Jackson, my teacher, one day when she came to find out why I don't come to school no more.

She was standing out in the yard, Big Ma on the porch, I'm peeping through the window.

"I need to know why Jessie Leigh isn't in school," said Amy Jackson.

"Ain't your business to know." This was Big Ma, puffing her pipe, dressed in overalls, manly shoes, as thin as a broom handle. "Jessie Leigh needs to be here helping me. She'll go back when I'm through with her."

"And when is that?"

"When I say when," said Big Ma, tapping the tobacco out of her pipe against the wall of the house. "Now get off my land cause I got work to do."

But I never do get to go back.

"Jessie Leigh! Jessie Leigh! Where you at, girl?"

That's Trish coming up in the yard. "Jessie Leigh," she holler.

"I'm in the kitchen," I holler back.

She standing in the doorway, looking at me, shaking her head. Her belly bigger than the last time I saw her. "Child, do you ever get tired of peeling peaches?"

"Sure I do," I tell her.

"Child, I wouldn't last."

"You would if you had to."

"I guess you right about that." She get herself a knife, drawing up a chair, and start helping me peel. "Your old mammy ain't coming home early, is she?"

"No," I say.

She quiet, like she don't believe what I just said. "Well. I hope not. I sure don't feel like cussing an old woman out early this morning."

I say nothing.

Trish—she my best friend. We used to be in school together until she got herself pregnant then got married to some old nigger who could be both our daddies and now they living down the road a piece on his land. Big Ma wouldn't like it if she knew Trish come over here every other day peeling around with her peaches while she gone to clean up Mrs. Massey's house. But Trish not care. Here she comes, wobbling up the road, hair neatly in ribbons and pigtails, down her back. A neat red or blue—but mostly red—summer dress that's always the same color as her ribbons. Matching socks, and a mighty fine pair of polished shoes, like she was going to church, but she was coming to see me.

"When you due?" I ask cause she's getting mighty big.

"Jessie Leigh, do you ever get tired of asking me that question?"

"I know, but you getting too big, like you ready to drop it any minute. Sure you ain't fixing to have twins?"

"Nope," she say real quick.

We quiet now, steady peeling peaches, humming to ourselves. I look out the window and it's still early—being maybe about ten or eleven o'clock and no more. The wind is blowing a little, not strong, but enough to make the corn stalks in Big Ma's garden sway. Real quiet—except for the faint sound of Mr. L.C. and his tractor from across the fields. Even Thomas playing quietly; I see him running or jumping past the window every so often. I look over at the barn and see Dudley scratching at the door, sniffing, then scratching some more. Foolish dog, I say to myself.

"This business is getting old." Trish drop her knife in her bowl. "Let's go sit out on the porch."

"I don't know about that. I can't take no break 'til noon. Big Ma will get me."

"Didn't you just say she ain't coming home early? Don't be a wench," she say smiling.

A cute breeze is blowing out here, us sitting on the porch. Thomas out in the yard playing, making mud pies and then squashing them with his feet and laughing up a storm, just having a good time. When he finally see us sitting out here, he comes running toward us, jumping on the porch with one big leap.

Trish: "Hey there, good looking."

I don't think he know what she said, but he flash that beautiful smile just the same. He look nothing like me. When folks see us walking into town with Big Ma, they say: "This your granddaughter?" But when they see Thomas, they say: "That child sure is yours. Look at them eyes!" Thomas' eyes. They big and brown—like our daddy's and grandmama's. Thomas is light brown, like our daddy's, like our grandmama's, with good hair. Not that kinky wool stuff that I got on my head.

But I look like the woman I've seen only once. My mama's tall, slinky like, real dark, like deep black coffee. She wasn't a good-looking thing, but the way she smiled, the way she threw her head back when she laughed, or the way she crossed her legs at the dinner table, or the twisty switchy way she walked, you wouldn't notice her ugliness. She wouldn't let you. Daddy met her in Chicago, just coming home from some war. She was some kind of singer-dancer or something. That's all I know about my mama, except I know Big Ma can't stand her and my daddy ain't with her no more. So I'm figuring, unlike me, my mama's something else.

"What's that crazy dog of yours doing, Jessie Leigh?"

I look over there by the barn and Dudley's scratching at the door, barking and sniffing, then scratching at the door some more.

"I don't know," I say. "Crazy dog."

Thomas sitting down by me, leaning his head against my leg. His soft curly hair feels good, like layers and layers of expensive silks trickling down his beautiful face, sometimes hiding those big beautiful eyes.

"I tell you what, if he's itching to get your mama's peaches, that dog got another thing coming." That's Trish.

"That dog know better. He don't bother them

peaches. A snake or something must be in there."

Thomas raise his head and run out to the barn where Dudley is. I follow behind him, and Trish—poor thing—is wobbling behind me. We all standing behind Dudley, who is steady scratching and carrying on. Then Thomas flips the latch and get ready to walk in, but I grab him by the back of his collar and he turn around and look at me and I shake my head no. Dudley start walking in, but he stop in the doorway and bark.

Me and Trish stick our heads in, looking around on the floor expecting to see a snake. But we see nothing, except for jars and jars of Big Ma's peaches sitting on the shelves that my daddy made for her before he left. We see nothing. We look over there by the metal barrels, by the plow and by the big sacks of feed, but we see nothing.

"We better go," say Trish, rubbing her big belly. "I don't want my baby coming out looking like a snake by the face."

I close the door, hooking the latch together, and we both walk back up to the porch. Thomas and Dudley, at first still at the door, but after awhile they go on.

"Whatever it is, Big Ma will find it and get it out," I say.

We sit for a long time, both of us forgetting the time, laughing and carrying on about school. Hardly nobody in my class liked me, except Trish. They made up a song for me and they sang it to make me cry. Trish say, "Don't you cry Jessie Leigh, they ain't nothing. Just nothing." But they sang their new song just for me:

Jessie Leigh, she so black
Blacker than me, blacker than you.
She so black 'til she's almost blue.

"Jessie Leigh, why you so quiet?"

"Huh?"

"Well," she say, "I best be making it back home. Curtis be home directly. "She raises herself out of the chair, moaning a little, and then, after finally standing up straight, thanks Jesus. "I'll see you, pudding."

"Bye." I stand and watch her as she wobble down the road. Thomas steady waving even though she not turn around. I go back in the house, start peeling my peaches again cause Big Ma will be home soon and if I don't have my ten quarts she going have a hissy fit on me. So I'm peeling real fast before she get here.

The hot sun's a fire orange as it sit over there behind the cotton fields, like the ground's afire. But it's cooler though, and quiet—peaceful like.

Big Ma's in the kitchen jarring the peaches I peeled today. She quiet, being since I done my ten quarts—thank you, sweet Jesus—before she got home. I'm sitting in the living room, just resting in the chair. Thomas in here with me, sprawled out on the floor, throwing his hands and arms out and up into the air like he trying to grab hold to the ceiling. I watch him.

Sometimes I get jealous of my brother—him being stone deaf and all. He ain't got to hear nobody fuss and cuss at him. And if they do, he just smile at them like he want to say, "I can't hear a word you said. So damn you." And he just fall out grinning. He's a lucky old thing.

"Jessie Leigh, didn't you hear me calling you, gal?"

I look up and Big Ma is standing over me with a dishrag in her hand like she fixing to smack me.

I hop out of the chair real quick, hoping she won't hit me.

"I swear, sometimes I think you worse off than he is," she say, nodding her head toward Thomas who's still over there on the floor trying to snatch the ceiling. "Take these out to the barn. And you bet' not break one jar."

So, I'm gathering up all the jars, scared—like always—about breaking one of Big Ma's jarred peaches but grabbing them quickly just the same. Suddenly, we hear a car coming up the road and I leave the jars right there on the table and go to the door to see who that is. We looking, Big Ma being the main one at the door, me and Thomas in the back.

And Lord, here come fat Sheriff Tucker in his car. He's coming up the road and the first thing Big Ma say is, "This here road sure can bring up some peculiar folks." Then here comes Dudley up from under the house, barking and snarling and letting Sheriff Tucker and his car know that this his territory.

"Y'all stay on the porch," say Big Ma, as she step off the porch, into the yard.

Thomas start to follow but I grab him by his arm and I hold on tight.

"Shut up, dog!" Big Ma stomping her feet, then Dudley get quiet.

"Mabel," he say, getting out the car, nodding his head, then spitting a wad of dip on the ground not too far from Dudley and Dudley growl because he don't like that spitting business one bit.

"Sheriff Tucker," Big Ma nod her head.

"Well, you know I wouldn't be here unless I got

important business, so I'll get right to it." He lean against the car, looking directly at Big Ma, who's looking directly back at him. "I'm looking for a speck of white trash that slithered through Harper sometime last night or night before. Seems like he got hold to some things at the General that didn't belong to him—including some of your peaches. He don't look much older that young'un" He's nodding at me. "Black hair, I think. Tall. Pretty close to the lean side. He got one of them slick Yankee ways of talking." He spits. "You seen him?"

Big Ma put her hands on her little hips: "I sho' did. Trampled up to my place last night, begging for water and food, and had the gumption to ask for a place to sleep. He wanted to come up into the house, but I tells him to get his dirty self off my place 'fore I sic this dog on him. That's what I gave him. And he left, too!" And with that, she grunts.

"Well, if you see him again, let me know 'cause he ain't getting away. We might let the dogs out but he's probably out of town by now. If he's smart." And with that, he turn the car around and ride off.

Inside, Big Ma say, "I don't want you going too far out of this yard, Jessie Leigh, while that trash is on the loose. No telling what's he's up to. That's all I need is for you to get ripe while I can barely keep food in you and Tom's mouth. You better see that Thomas stay in the house while I'm gone. And if I catch you out past them peach trees in the yard, I'll skin you. If I catch Thomas outside while I'm gone, I'll still skin you. You hear, gal?"

"Yes, ma'am."

"Now, take them peaches to the barn like I told you."

"Yes, ma'am." I'm walking toward the barn with big Ma's crate of jarred peaches.

These peaches. If it wasn't for these peaches us probably be starved to death, or naked or both. There's ten spotting the backyard; ten in the front, five on each side of the road leading all the way up the house. On Saturdays, us pick peaches most all day out in the hot sun, sweating and carrying on. Then everyday next week, I peel peaches. Peel and peel. Then when Big Ma get home from work she cut them up and get them ready to be jarred, and when she through jarring them, I take them out to the barn with the others. Then one day, when the barn's good and tight, she load them up in the wagon, hitch the horse up and take them to town to sell to the General Merchandising store. Everybody loves Big Ma peaches.

My granddaddy planted these trees. Before he left

me, he say, "You as sweet as these here peaches."
That was my granddaddy.

I set the crate down next to the barn while I open
up the door. When I finally get in, I close the door
behind me to keep Dudley out who just loves sniffling around in here. I put the crate on the shelf
and start taking the jars out. But suddenly—dear
Lord—suddenly, I hear something move behind
me and I'm too scared to turn around to look at
whatever it is. I know it ain't no snake; snake don't
make this loud of noise. I keep still, hoping it will
go away. I'm still holding a jar in my hand, since I'm
too scared to set it down for fear that it might make
whatever it is mad. It moves again, and it sounds
like it's getting closer and I start shaking. It's getting
closer. And closer. And...

Quickly, I turn around to see what's about to
kill me. And there it is, looking right at me and me
looking back and I'm so scared I feel pee coming
down my legs.

"Hi," he say.

He starts walking toward me, but I move back,
though I can't go nowhere since I'm backed up
against the shelf. He smile and stretch out his hand
toward me.

"I ain't going to hurt you, Jessie Leigh."

Finally, I say weakly, "Ain't you the white trash they looking for?" He look a whole lot different though—cleaner, clean clothes, and his hair been cut.

He quit smiling. "Yep." He drops his hand down to his side. "But I didn't do what they said I did. I heard that fat sheriff tell your grandmother that I stole from that old store in town. I didn't do it." He sits down on a pile of hay pouting.

I still hadn't move being since I still ain't too sure about him.

Suddenly, he say, "You going to tell I'm here?"

"No."

"You are."

"I ain't."

"You are."

"Okay, watch and see."

He lie back on the hay, arms folded behind his head, looking up at me. I'm watching him back. He looks a whole lot different than from the last time I saw him. He ain't wearing them baggy ragged shirt and pants. He got on a pair of denims and a red flannel shirt. His black hair bounces every time he talk. Charcoal eyes he has, along with a thick pair of eyebrows and eyelashes. He's the darkest white boy I ever seen; his skin's a deep rich tan brown.

"They thinking about sending the dogs after you when daylight get here."

"I doubt it. They think I'm way out of town by now. You got anything to eat?"

"You ought to be already full," I say, us both looking at the empty jars of peaches lying on the barn floor not too far from where he's stretched out.

He look shamed. "Well, they were good but they did nothing for me. I need some real food."

"I can bring you something tonight when Big Ma go to bed."

"Thank you, Jessie Leigh." He looks relieved. Finally, he sit up and starts staring at me again. "You're pretty," he say.

I put my hands over my mouth and giggle.

"Why you laughing? You don't think so?"

I'm steady giggling because it's really funny.

"I think..."

"Jessie Leigh! What you doing in that barn, gal? Bring your tail out of there!"

I stop laughing. Big Ma was hollering at me. At first, it sounds like she was hollering from the porch, but then it sounds like she was steady coming toward the barn. I get scared. "Here I come," I holler. "I got to go," I tell him.

"I see you tonight," he says, reaching out toward

me but I'm already heading for the door with the empty crate in my hand, making sure the door's lock.

Inside, Big Ma holler at me, saying I'm not well up there and almost making me cry but I run to my pallet and hide my face in the pillow cause I'm real sad. I put myself in a ball on my pallet and cry. I'm crying all by myself, cause even the moon ain't out tonight.

When I wake up, it's dark, the moon still not out. I wait and listen for any noise, but I hear nothing. I get up and put some clothes on. I tip over to the other side of the room and pull back the large bedspread that's hanging on a rope that separates my half of the room with Thomas's. He sleep. I tip to the kitchen. I find two biscuits in the icebox, and several mixed pieces of squirrel and possum meat. On the floor, next to the box, I get the small jar of honey and slip out the door.

"Gone dog," I say to Dudley, who trying to sniff at what I got in my hands. He leaves.

He jump up when he see me come in and help me set the stuff down on the ground.

"I didn't think you were coming."

"I said I was, didn't I?"

Already, he poking the foods in his mouth, sticking the meats between the cold biscuits and dipping it all in the jar of honey. I'm sitting not too far from him; he's going to town on eating. When he through, he drink the juice from a jar of peaches, wiping his mouth with his shirt. "Thank you," he say.

"You welcome," I say. I'm staring at his head. He got pretty hair.

"What's on my head?"

"Nothing." I'm shamed. "You got pretty hair."

He smile, almost blush, and I wished I didn't say that. He scoot closer to where I'm sitting and touch my arm. I jump, move back, hide my face with my hands.

"Why are you doing that?"

"I'm shamed," I say.

"Shamed? Why?"

"I don't know," hunching my shoulders, still hiding.

He grab my arm, trying to pull my hands off my face, but I'm almost stronger. "Don't do that," he say. "Don't hide your face. He jerk my hands and look right into my face. "I like you Jessie Leigh."

I start laughing.

He smile. "What's so funny?"

I'm laughing some more and I can't stop. "You can't be liking me."

"Why not?"

I'm steadying laughing, almost losing my breath. "You can't be liking me 'cause..." I might be laughing—I don't know—but I feel real sad again, so I must be crying, or about to. "You can't be liking me cause I'm a black gal." And then I know I'm crying cause I feel my face getting wet.

He hug me hard and I can't stop crying. Then he look down at me and kiss me. Not on my jaw, but on my lips. Dear Lord! I don't know what to say or do. I never been kissed by a white boy. Black boy, either. One time I was almost kissed by Johnny Parker, this boy who used to be in school with me. But he's a nasty boy. His daddy threw him out the house when he caught him putting his thing in one of the milking cows. I wouldn't let him kiss me for nothing. Nasty boy!

He kiss me again. Then again. I might be kissing him back, but I ain't too sure. I touch him and he touch me and we touching each other all over. I hear that dog, whatever his name is, and I say, get away dog, but not loud enough.

I am always wondering all the time what it's like to touch up on boys. Now I'm wondering what he look like naked. I know what naked boys look like. I seen Thomas one time, but he don't really count being since he's my brother.

"I think I love you, Jessie Leigh," he say, kissing me.

"What's your name?" I ask, kissing him back.

It's almost daylight when I wake up. I look over at Eddie and he's still sleep. I put my clothes on and slip out the door.

I lay down on my pallet, but I not sleep. I lie here watching the sun come up. Soon, Big Ma will be getting up and going to Mrs. Massey's house. I'll have to get up after a while and start peeling peaches. I smell my arm and I can smell Eddie. I try going asleep with my arm across my nose.

I'm almost asleep when I hear something far away: barking. Then I hear Big Ma's feet hitting the floor. By the time both of us get to the door, we see Eddie busting out the barn and running toward Mr. L.C.'s cotton field. Big Ma hollering, "Get him! Get him!" and I'm screaming and crying. I holler his name when the dogs bring him down.

When the men bring him back through the yard, he say my name: "Jessie Leigh" They tell him to shut up, but he don't. And they ride off on their horses, dragging Eddie behind them, down the road, out of sight.

Then later on Big Ma come walking in the house

with a big stick and she beat me with it, asking me how that boy get to liking me. But I'm laughing while she beating me cause I'm sick of being sad. And she beats until she get tired; and I laugh until I get tired; now we both lying out on the floor breathing hard.

Me and Trish just sitting out here on the porch now. I'm peeling peaches. She holding her new baby, trying to make it get quiet, but he steady squalling. I stop peeling and she give him to me. I unloosen my blouse and start feeding him. He quiet now, lips smacking.

We call this baby Luke. It used to be my baby until Big Ma put it up for sale since she say I ain't too right in the head to have no baby. Trish and her husband bought him for three hundred dollars after her first one come out dead.

Sometimes, Trish come over and share my baby with me. Big Ma don't care, being since she say I'm spoiled now anyway.

I feel the cool breeze where the baby is feeding. I look down at him. He look up at me. He look just like his daddy. A whole lot like his mama. The sweet thing.

THE WITNESS TREE

The sun ain't up yet when I wake this morning, but I still don't hear Big Ma in the kitchen. I don't even smell bacon tickling my nose. I get up and put my clothes on, then I peep over the hanging quilt to see if Thomas is still sleeping in his bed. But he not there.

I go to the kitchen, but they're not there, everything looking the same way as it was yesterday.

I go to Big Ma room—it's sort of dark in here 'cause the sun steady trying to come up—and I see her sleeping in her bed. And there's Thomas, looking like a graveyard ghost, sitting on her bed, shaking her real hard even though she not move. I just stand in the doorway and look. Thomas steady shaking and don't stop until he see me, then he get off the bed and run and grab hold of me.

We go to her bed and I bend down and shake her, just like Thomas did. But when she don't wake, I put my head next to her arm and start crying. I'm crying so hard that it looks like it's raining in Big Ma

43

bedroom. Thomas—he start pulling all over me like he don't know why I'm crying. "Big Ma dead," I tell him. But I don't know why I say this, being since he's stone deaf and can't hear what I just said. "Big Ma dead," I say again, just in case he can hear. He put his head down next to mine and he cry, too.

I go put on my clothes and get Thomas ready and we start walking down the road. Not too long before we see Trish house and see her sitting on the porch. I holler her name.

Trish look up, see it's me, and start smiling. She put down her bowl of peas and holler my name back: "Jessie Leigh!"

Thomas already run up in the yard and hugging her. I start crying when Trish look at me. She start running at me, but then she forget about the baby and go back and pick him up, then she come out here to me.

"Big Ma dead," I say. "She didn't wake up when I shake her this morning. I didn't hear her in the kitchen. Big Ma dead," I say again just in case she didn't hear me the first time. We hug each other, the baby in the middle. Trish—she my best friend.

We go inside—Thomas already in here playing with Mr. Curtis. Mr. Curtis is Trish husband. He's real old; I don't know how much, but his hair is starting to turn white.

"Hi, there, Jessie Leigh."

"Hi," I say, and that's all I say cause I'm steady wanting to cry some more.

"Miss Mabel just passed," Trish tell him.

"Oh."

Me and Thomas stay up at Trish house all day today. Later on, Mr. Curtis gone up to the square—to drink probably, which is something he always doing when he ain't sleep. He took Thomas with him cause he likes Thomas and Thomas likes him.

We sitting in her kitchen sewing Big Ma's passing gown. Trish main one talking—talking about getting Big Ma ready for her wake. "I'll get Curtis to build Miss Mabel a nice box," she say. But I still say nothing.

When we finish up Big Ma's gown, they come home—Mr. Curtis as drunk as he want to be, just like Trish said. "Hi, y'all," Mr. Curtis say, tipping a hat off his head like he never been inside his own house before.

"Fool." That's Trish.

But here come Thomas, and he wobbling, too.

Trish jump up out of her seat. "Curtis, has Thomas been drinking?

"No."

Trish grab Thomas and smell his breath. "He has! What kind of fool do you think I am, Curtis?"

"I don't know, baby," Mr. Curtis say. "What kind you want to be?"

"Don't you mock me, Curtis Brownlee Taylor. I'll scratch your damn eyes out."

He laugh some more, then grab and hug her.

"Don't you touch me!" But she laughing, too.

I look at them and I smile, but then I look over at Thomas and get sick cause he just threw up on the floor.

"Lord." That's what Trish say.

Later on, Trish make popcorn for us to eat and after that we go to bed. I lay awake listening to the night, then I think about how Big Ma doing. The last thing I hear tonight is Mr. Curtis making a heap of noise—as drunk as he still is—steady hammering away on Big Ma's box.

This morning me and Trish and Thomas get ready to go up to our house to get Big Ma ready. Before we leave, she try to get in touch with my daddy who's living in Memphis, but she can't find him.

Trish go behind her house and get that rusty—it used to be red, but it's old now—that rusty wagon that we used to ride each other in long time ago. We put the box across it and head on down the road.

Thomas pulling the wagon cause that's something he likes doing. Me and Trish hold the box at each end so it won't fall off, being since this road is real bumpy.

Before we can get up in the yard good, here comes Dudley out from under the house and get to barking. But when he see who it is, he comes out here with us. Thomas let go of the wagon and run off with Dudley. So, I got to pull and guide the wagon the rest of the way home almost all by myself being since Trish really can't help too good cause she steady holding the baby.

Inside, me and Trish stand around Big Ma's bed. I'm scared to look so I cover up my face. But when Trish pull back the cover I have to look. She don't look scary; she look like she sleeping.

"Go get some hot soapy water and a towel so I can wash up Miss Mabel."

I go make the water. When I get back, Trish got Big Ma naked. I stand and look. She look like a little monkey with no hair. I look so hard 'til Trish say, "Hurry up, baby."

While Trish washing Big Ma, I go get Thomas and we go bring the box in the house and set it on the kitchen table.

"Go find a nice clean sheet and line up the box,"

Trish say.

I go outside and get the bedspread that Big Ma hung day before yesterday. Thomas come over here by me and both of us carry the bedspread back inside the house, holding it up real high so it won't get dirty.

We put the spread in the box. I'm doing the spreading cause Thomas just run outside.

I go back in the bedroom and Trish already got Big Ma in her gown. Trish got Big Ma hair made up real good; her face cleaned up real good, too, so the light hit it nicely and make this pretty shine being since Big Ma always had good skin anyway.

"Big Ma look pretty," I say.

"She sure does." That's Trish. "Where's the box?"

"Kitchen table," I say.

"Okay, help me get Miss Mabel in there. Here, grab her legs."

I do, even though I don't want to, but I do anyway. She feel funny; she feel cold. Not cold cold. But just cold. She so little that I could have, or Trish could have picked her up all by ourselves, not weighing no more than a big basket of peaches.

We in the kitchen now and then we lift her up and try putting her over into the box. She don't fit this way, so we turn her this way. But she don't fit this way, either. We keep moving her in and out of the box until Big Ma hair come undone. Finally, we find out that Big Ma won't fit in her box at all. So Trish holler out, "That damn Curtis Taylor made this box too damn narrow!"

I might been sleeping for a long time cause I wake up at Thomas shaking me, and when I open my eyes, I see him looking at me real scared. When he see me see him, he gets real happy and hug me.

Later on this afternoon I go outside and get the wagon and start pulling it down the road, Thomas walking with me. Then Dudley see us walking and he come running out here, barking and jumping around cause he real happy.

And here I go walking—Thomas and Dudley just jumped in the wagon and I'm pulling them. Town ain't far, so it ain't long before we get on the main road that will take us where we going.

This road mighty bumpy; the wagon jumping everywhere every time it hit a rock or go down off in a hole, making Thomas and Dudley jiggle around inside the wagon—but we steady go on and not stop.

I hear a car or truck coming up behind us. I don't turn around though. I will wait 'til it get up next to us. Dudley barking up a fine storm now, which making Thomas look at whoever it is. I look over and see Mrs. Massey—this nice white lady Big Ma use to work for.

"Jessie Leigh," she say, "I just came from your house yesterday. Where's your grandmother? Is she sick?"

"No, ma'am," I say. "She ain't sick."

"Then why hasn't she been to work?"

"She dead. She didn't wake up and I didn't smell no bacon in the kitchen and then—hush up dog!—and then we got ready and went up to Trish house."

"Who is Trish?"

"Trish—she my best friend."

"Where is she now?"

"She gone home to cuss Mr. Curtis out."

"No, Jessie Leigh. I mean your grandmother. Where is your grandmother."

I say, "She on her bed now."

"Now? Where was she at first?"

"On the table," I say.

She look at me for a long time, then look at Dudley, lying down in the wagon breathing real hard from all that barking; then she look at Thomas, who steady sticking his tongue out and making faces at Mrs. Massey. She breathed out real hard and then she say, "Jessie Leigh, why was your grandmother on the table?"

"We was trying to put her in her box, but Mr. Curtis made the box too little cause he been drinking too much. Now Trish gone to cuss him out. She say she be back though."

For a long time she don't say nothing again. Then: "I got to go over in Madison County, but I'll be back late this evening to see Miss Mabel. Hear?"

"Yes, ma'am," I say, and that's all I say cause I'm tired of talking and ready to get into town.

"Bye," she say, then she drive off bringing up all this dust off the road, making Dudley bark all over again, making me and Thomas squint and rub our eyes.

For a moment, we blind the dust so thick; but then the dust start clearing up and we can see, so we steady tread on.

I leave the wagon on the sidewalk and go in the General, walking through the door they got for us in the back, leaving Dudley in the wagon nodding, Thomas holding my hand cause he not too sure about this place.

This place—Harper's General Merchandising Store—smell good. It smell like Christmas: candy and apples and oranges and a heap of spices, foods and stuff.

"May I help y'all? My shelves full of peaches if you coming to sell me some more." This here Mr. Harper. He own this store. He used to buy my Big Ma's jarred peaches.

"No, sir. I ain't selling no peaches."

"Then what you want?""

"A box."

"A box? What kind of box?"

"A big box," I say.

"What you going to put in your big box?"

"My grandmama," I say, getting tired of him asking me all these questions.

"Your grandmama? Who? Mabel?"

"Yes, sir," I say. "She didn't wake up instead of cooking breakfast, then I got ready and went and got Trish so she could...but Mr. Curtis box he made was too little and Trish say..." I'm about to cry, so I get quiet. I cover up my face with one of my hands so he won't see me cry; my other hand I'm steady holding onto Thomas.

For a long time he don't say nothing either, then he go: "You go outside, out back, by that big pile of wood. There's two crates I just put out there yesterday that Mr. and Mrs. Campbell's coffee tables came in. You get yourself one of those and—is that your old rusty wagon out there where that dog is?"

"Yes, sir," I say, steady trying to hide my face.

"Okay, you get yourself one of them crates and put it across that wagon you got and you put Mabel in that. Hear?"

"Yes, sir." I don't move, but steady standing there hiding my face and holding Thomas hand.

"Go on and do like I say. Mabel ain't getting no fresher."

Me and Thomas hurry on out the store.

We back on the road with the crate on our wagon. I'm pulling, Thomas holding the crate. We ain't on this bumpy road a long time when one of the wheels pop off and the wagon turn over. I try putting it back on, but it keep popping off, so I leave it in the road. Now, me and Thomas got to switch up: he doing the pulling now, and I'm bending over holding up the wagon where the wheel used to be and we bring Big Ma's new box on home with us.

I clean it out real good, then I line it up with the same bedspread. I go get her and put her in her box. She fit real good.

"Jessie Leigh! Where you at?"

"I'm in the kitchen," I holler back at Trish. I'm standing beside Big Ma so I can see how happy Trish going to get when she see that Big Ma got a new box.

I hear Trish coming, she already talking even though she not in here yet. "I still can't get hold of your daddy and Curtis is going to make another box and folks are going to be coming to Miss Mabel's waking so we need to clean this place up before..." She stop when she get to the kitchen, looking at me, then looking at Big Ma. She look like she might cry, even though there's nothing to cry about. Finally, Trish say, "Miss Mabel's new box looks just fine. Just fine."

I'm happy.

Our house packed. Folks from everywhere here. There's Miss Fannie Taylor and her twin sister Miss Frances. Miss Annabelle, Mr. Cook and his wife Mrs. Cook. Mr. Ford, and his oldest, Eva. Mr. and Mrs. Williams—that's Sonny Buck's mama and daddy, Terry's mama and daddy—Terry here, too with his bad self—Miss Linda, Miss Teresa Jackson, and a heap of other folks I don't know.

They brung food. It's so much food in big Ma's room 'til every time I go back there to peep at it I get dizzy. So I quit doing that.

In the kitchen, the older folks sitting around Big Ma talking every now and then 'til somebody get to singing church songs, even though Big Ma wasn't the churching kind, but they sing anyway.

Me and Trish—we got the kitchen looking real nice—plenty of candles everywhere so it look real holy like.

Miss Frances walk in the kitchen—she wearing this real loud purple dress—she walk in the kitchen and look over in Big Ma's face. She look like she might cry she looking so sad. Then she step back and read what's on the side of Big Ma's box: THIS END UP. "THIS END UP? Hell, don't y'all know which way this woman suppose to go in the ground?"

I start crying. Trish tell me to be quiet. She tell Miss Frances to shut up.

"I didn't mean nothing by that," she tell everybody. "You know, I buried my Reggie several years back. Dead folks don't mind you having a little fun."

"Now, how do you know?" This Miss Taylor, Miss Frances sister.

"Cause Reggie told me."

"Frances, quit your lying."

"I ain't lying, girl. I talk to Reggie all the time. He used to scare me, but I'm used to him now. He's a damn good spook. That's cause I gave him a good waking. We sang, we danced—hell, we had a ball. That's how you make good with the folks on the other side"

"Ah, Frances," say her sister, "you talking foolishness. Hush up and sit down somewhere, now."

"No, I ain't talking crazy, either. Remember Sam Davis? That crazy fellow in Madison County with that funny walk?"

"Yeah," everybody say.

"Well, how y'all think he got to walking like that?"

Mr. Ford say, "He fell out of a tree cause he been drinking."

"Nope," Miss Frances shaking her head, making sure nobody say different. "That's what he tell everybody to keep from telling the truth. You remember Raymond Brown? That big black nigger that used to live up there on old man Rabbit's place?"

Everybody say yeah.

"Well. Sam Davis owed him some money and he never did get around to paying Raymond. And when Raymond died of pneumonia Sam said now he don't have to pay Raymond that money back. Well, about two years later, you can just imagine who came knocking on Sam Davis' door one night just as bold as he want to be."

"Who?" I holler out.

"Raymond Brown," Miss Frances holler back.

"Frances, you lying!"

"No, I ain't," her eyes getting bigger. "He told Sam to give him his money he owe him. Course, Sam as scared as he want to be, but he tell Raymond that he ain't about to give good money to a man who been dead for two years."

"Then what happened?" I ask.

"What you think happened? Sam Davis got his ass smacked by a damn spook. Smacked his head so hard 'til his head is tilted to one side to this day. That's why he walk so funny, he thinks the ground is crooked and not his head."

"Hush up, Frances," her sister say again, "you not doing nothing but talking crazy."

"Well, believe me if you want to." And that's all Miss Frances say about that.

We sit for a long time helping Big Ma pass on through. Tonight we bury her. Mr. Curtis already dug a grave out there under the biggest peach tree in our front yard. Trish already been out checking to see if it's big enough.

It ain't a big tree, but it got a whole big field by itself. It look like it is looking at us, like it's trying to figure out what in the world we doing, digging a big hole where it is standing and dropping stuff off in there—probably on its feet—then we standing around it doing nothing but looking down at the thing we just put in the ground. Or, this tree remember me and my brother Thomas and my Big Ma picking peaches off its branches everyday, every summer—and now it's real sad, too. It look real sad, even though it is dark out here (some folks got flashlights, holding it for Mr. Curtis who steady packing the dirt on Big Ma) you can see the branches and they drooping over like they weeping. Yes, it's sad, too. Mrs. Massey drive up and she come stand out here by the grave with us, everybody looking at her real hard cause she's the only one who ain't black like it's her fault.

The preacher man say a few words, I can't remember what cause I'm now crying. Trish and Miss Frances try to hush me up, but I'm steady crying. Thomas holding my hand and he crying, too.

After a while, we come on back up to the house. Now everybody start eating, but I go to my room and look out the window where Big Ma at now. The tree look like it is watching the grave, then it look like it is looking at me, too—real sad like. I look at this tree for a long time, then I lay down on my bed cause I'm real tired and real sleepy. Later on tonight, I feel somebody trying to get me up and make me eat, but I don't get up. Before falling off to sleep again, I think about Big Ma, but I'm figuring she's being watched over now.

Jerome Wilson

SNOW ON CHRISTMAS

My sister Maggie ain't got no sense at all when it comes to Santa Claus and Christmas and stuff because every year around this time she get all nervous and strung out and about to bust full of tears cause she said she is scared tee-totally to death about some fat white man tipping through our house while we sleeping. She not even caring he is toting us presents. And it already being two days before Christmas so my ears are steady getting worn out by her constant yack-yack-yacking for the last several weeks or so about Santa Claus.

"Suppose I wake up and see him and he standing right over my bed looking at me?"

"Why he got to look at you for?" I asked her, steady trying to figure out if my sister is really all there or is she really just a scared six year old. I don't know. "He ain't got no reason to be looking at you. He's too busy. Suppose he stopped and looked at every person he brought presents for? Nobody would be getting nothing cause Christmas would be over

61

and done by the time he finished peeping at folks."

"Well, I'm scared."

I just rolled my eyes in the back of my head cause I can't believe we having this conversation. "Santa Claus don't want you," I tell her, but she ain't believing a word I said.

Last year, she was scared that his reindeers were going to break in and bite at her feet under the covers. She wore shoes to bed for days. The year before that, she believed she was going to get snatched by Santa and taken to the North Pole and be put to work in his toy factory. My sister got problems.

Of course, I know the real deal about Santa Claus. Learned all about that situation along with where babies come from and why come you ain't suppose to ask a lady her age. But I don't tell Maggie about Santa Claus cause Mama made me promise not to tell her nothing about it. And she even made me some banana nut muffins—they my favorite—so I had to keep quiet cause I wanted the muffins to keeping coming. Which I don't understand cause grown folks are always telling us that we better tell the truth and it ain't right to lie, then they turn right around and give you muffins so you don't tell nobody the truth. I don't like to be tricked in a trickified way. It ain't right.

So, anyways, here we go sitting outside on the curb talking to Monica and Junebug—they brother and sister—who are on the other side of the street sitting on their curb on account Mama and Daddy tell me and Maggie we can't have no company. They always telling us nobody can come over and play and we can't go nowhere either. So, I sit on the street curb all the time and talk to whoever is walking by. I used to hate it, can't go running off and all of that, especially when Kicky or Barry and Wayne come riding by and try to get me to go off to where the latest building is going up so we can ride over the dirt mounds with our bikes. Or maybe we can find some big planks and make ramps and do some Evel Knievals. Or Barry sneaked some naked lady books out from under his daddy's nose for us to go around the house and look at. I never go cause I know Daddy will get me. In fact, we can't go pass that big dogwood tree that I like to climb that sit two houses down on our side of the street. But I don't care. Sometimes I just haul my homework—books, paper, pencil and all—right out here on the curb with me and work on it. Sometimes they talk about us, saying our Mama and Daddy are stone cold crazy and don't let us do nothing, but I don't care. They make Maggie cry. I tell her to hush up, but she just get louder.

So, Junebug, who always been having a big mouth ever since he started off in the fifth grade with me, is steady moaning on about what he getting for Christmas and we listening and saying *ooo* and *ahh* even though I don't really care because I know he lying. Always lying. He get the same amount of stuff everybody else in the neighborhood get—except for Rico cause his daddy is a real life gangster like in the movies and always got a wad of money as thick as my fist—but Junebug don't care. He just got to lie.

Of course, Maggie ask out loud, not asking nobody special, but just asking anybody whoever want to answer: "Ain't y'all scared Santa Claus gonna be looking at y'all when you sleeping?"

I roll my eyes and say "damn" under my breathe cause I don't want Maggie telling Mama and Daddy I've been cussing again.

"Aw, shit, what's wrong with you? There ain't no Santa." Then Junebug look over at me and say, "What's the hell wrong with your sister, Sonny Buck?"

I hunch my shoulders. I declare I don't know.

"There ain't no Santa Claus. It's your damn mama and daddy who be bringing you toys at night."

Monica shake her head in agreement with her

brother. "Uh-huh. And if you living with your damn grandmama, it's her."

Maggie look over at me, frowning up like she don't know what is going on and looking like she just might bawl and cry, eyes watering up and her bottom lip shaking like Jell-O. "It ain't no Santa Claus?" steady looking at me and just waiting for my answer, me knowing if it's the wrong answer, she's going to bawl.

I look up in the sky to see if it's going to snow or something or anything so I don't have to look at Maggie. I'm thinking why I got to lie and carry on when any fool can tell you there ain't no Santa Claus.

"No," I say. "There ain't no damn Santa Claus. There never was. He died a long time ago. Heart attack probably."

At first, I thought she was going to be calm about the whole matter. She just sat there, like when you get smacked across the face and been told that you better not cry. It was like that. But the next thing we know, she's screaming like a monkey, getting in the wind for the house hollering for Mama and Daddy like the boogie-man after her. I just shake my head.

Monica and Junebug rolling all over each other they laughing so. I can't stand them sometimes.

After a while, Daddy holler my name. I get sick all over cause I know Maggie done told all that she could tell and then some. I feel like not moving, but he calling my name again so I figure I better go.

"You better go see what your daddy want with you," say Junebug, real serious like cause everybody in my neighborhood know my Daddy don't play.

So, I go on up to the house and I see him in the door with his head hanging out and the first thing he say to me when I get into hearing distance: "What you say to Maggie?" He frowning up like he been sleeping or something and just been made mad about being woke up.

I look down at the ground cause I ain't too sure what I should be saying, but then I'm figuring it really don't matter none. So, I better be careful about the whole thing so I can at least not get one as hard. "I don't know," I say, cause I ain't too sure what I should be saying or how to say it.

"You don't know?" Daddy laughing at me, just dying laughing—not cause I'm funny, but cause he can't believe what I just said. "You don't know? Boy, you can't remember what you said to make Maggie cry?" He look at me.

I stand there and look at a leaf on the ground. I wish I was that leaf.

"Answer me, boy!"

"I..."

"What?"

"I don't..."

"What? Speak up, boy!"

"I don't know."

"Yes, you do know."

I wait awhile; maybe he'll forget I'm standing there in the yard in front of him. Maybe if he look at me hard enough I'll just slowly disappear or get transported onto another planet and not have to answer his question.

"Now, if I got to ask you one more time..."

"I told her it wasn't no more Santa Claus. Santa Claus is dead."

He looked at me with nothing on his face, so I don't know if he mad or sad—but I know he ain't happy.

I look back at the leaf on the ground. The wind started blowing and the leaf rolled away.

"Come here."

I don't move.

"Boy, are you deaf as well as stupid, too?"

I walk up on the porch where he standing.

"Now, what did you say you said?"

"I said..."

He smack me off the porch. The grass is hard and cold, and my face feel like it ain't on my head it's hurting so. But I feel like staying here for the rest of my life and never get up.

* * *

Tonight is Christmas Eve. I'm happy and excited. Even Maggie is happy too now that she know Santa Claus won't be looking at her on account he's been deader than a doorknob for years and years. She keep asking me when he die and where he buried at and what he die of, but I tell her that I wasn't at his damn funeral so I don't know nothing.

Mama and Daddy gone to a Christmas party. They told us not to open the door for nobody and don't pick up the phone unless it ring twenty times cause that mean that it's them calling us.

Soon they out the door me and Maggie tear up the house looking for presents. The closets, under beds, under cabinets, behind couches and here and there and over there and back here again. Nothing. We don't find nothing. We always find them, but not this time.

Now Maggie thinking I been lying about the whole thing. There really is a Santa Claus. That's why we can't find no presents cause he ain't brought them yet. I don't say nothing.

We sit and watch *The Muppet Show* and then later on tonight Maggie get sleepy and I help her get in bed. Seems like soon she under the covers she already sleeping.

I go back and watch tv some more. It's getting real late. I don't know what time it is, but it's getting real late cause I ain't never seen any of these tv shows I'm looking at.

I get scared. Maybe Mama and Daddy got in a car wreck and now they laying out in the bushes and nobody know where they at. Maybe some bad people stole them and got them tied up with rope in some house that nobody ain't been living in for years and years. Or maybe they get shot up in the head, so me and Maggie won't have no more Mama or Daddy and we got to live with some folks we don't know who will make us eat grits without no sugar and butter.

I sit in the dark and wait and wait and wait. I keep looking out the window but I don't see no car that look like ours. I don't see no cars at all. Now I'm real scared and now I know something done happened cause they would call.

I start crying. Not a loud hollering screaming

crying like Maggie always doing, but a quiet cry so nobody can hear me but me and I can only hear me from my insides cause I don't make no noise at all. I don't know how long I sit, but I know it's a long time. Just about all of the channels on the tv got the stripped color bar things on them now it's so late. It don't matter none anyways. I sit and wait and wait and wait. I try to think happy things, but when you get all down to it, it's still dark and scary and you still by yourself.

All of a sudden the door open up and the living room lights clicking on so fast and bright until you got to squint to see. They finally came home: Mama leaning on Daddy and Daddy leaning on Mama and they both leaning on each other trying to get through the door at the same time but get their legs tangled up with each other and then they laugh. Holler out. They both finally squirt inside the house bumping and banging and laughing. Then they see me sitting over in the corner.

"Why you crying?" Mama asked, frowning up, eyes looking shiny like she got lit light bulbs screwed in her eye sockets. She sit down in the chair next to the big Christmas tree.

"I ain't crying," I say, cutting my eyes at Daddy. I try wiping my eyes and face so they can't see how wet it is.

"What you crying for, boy?" Daddy asked, stepping closer to the couch where I been sitting and waiting.

"I ain't crying," I say again, trying to sound like I ain't never heard of crying.

He grab me by my arms and picked me up so we looking face to face. "Listen, you little bastard. Don't you lie to me. Don't you lie to me."

He shake me hard until my head is moving back and forth and my neck is hurting. He smell like all kinds of alcohol drinkings.

"Hey! Leave him alone," say Mama, jumping out of the chair, but she jump too hard and lost her balance and she fall backwards into the Christmas tree, busting and bending ornaments, and her and the tree fall on the floor. She don't wake up, but just say, "good night, folks. You were wonderful!" and keep on sleeping right there next to the tree.

Daddy throw me back on the couch. "Take your little ass to bed!"

I run.

I hear him holler at me, "You ain't getting shit for Christmas! You hear me? Not shit!"

I get to my room and get under the covers and stay. I don't sleep, I just stay still under the covers. I lie there for a long time. I don't know how long, but after a while I start seeing pieces of the sun come up and the room get brighter and brighter. Pretty soon, I hear Maggie in her room getting out of bed and going in the living room to see her presents. I don't get up.

I hear Maggie laughing and hollering and ripping paper. She run in my room to wake me up. I pretend like I'm too sleepy to go look at presents. I don't want to look at the living room. I tell her to go away. But she steady bothering me. She pulling all over my arm. I pull back. But she pull harder. Finally, I get up cause I'm sick of her yanking on my arm and whining about Christmas and presents.

We go to the living room and there is the tree, sitting up and shining and glittering with stuff under it. The tree ain't on the floor; Mama ain't on the floor either—everything looking the same like nothing ever happened. I guess Daddy straightened everything out, but I don't know and I don't care.

Maggie give me a present with my name on it. I just look at it.

"Open it, fool," she say smiling.

I do. It's two Evel Knievel motorcycles with action figures.

We sit around and I watch Maggie open one present after another. Then I'm watching the Christmas parade on TV and I wonder why come all these folks got to be walking down the street parading and waving and not at home opening presents. I change the channel to see Roadrunner and the Coyote. They're more fun.

We hear the bedroom door slowly creak open and Daddy slowly walk out holding his head. Maggie run up to him and show him her new house shoes.

"Yeah, yeah, that's nice. Go play somewhere." He slowly drag on to the bathroom, but then he suddenly say, "Sonny Buck, you might have gotten more if you had believed in Santa Claus." Then he close the door and start throwing up, heaving and cussing.

For the rest of the day I play with my motorcycles and Maggie sit around putting new clothes on her doll and wearing her new house shoes all at the same time.

I see on the tv that the weatherman say it might snow. I tell Maggie. Tonight me and Maggie keep peeping out of the window. We sit and watch for the snow. Mama—who finally woke up—made me and Maggie popcorn and we sit in the window smacking on popcorn and waiting. Suddenly, it start raining—at first, real soft, then harder.

"Oh!" is what Maggie say. "Where's the snow?"

I say nothing.

No snow on Christmas, but just cold hard raindrops beating on the house and at the window at us. Maggie is real tired and ready for Christmas to be over now. Me, too. She fall asleep next to me, still wearing her new house shoes. I sit for a while making sure the rain don't turn to snow. It never do nothing but keep raining. All night long it keep going and going and it don't stop. Finally, I yawn and lay my head down and sleep, too.

THE DISAPPEARANCE OF
MISS TAMMY FAYE LOVEJOY

Tammy Faye Lovejoy twirled up on the porch of Luther's General Store where Willy and Elroy were sitting playing checkers while drinking grape Nehi and announced that she was going to go far away from here. But they paid her no never mind because Tammy had been saying that almost going on ten years now, ever since her mama died, so the threat was pretty much no good anymore.

Neither men said anything, but Tammy didn't wait for an answer, but twirled off the porch—she had always wanted to be a dancer she said—and continued on down the old dusty road making the bend in such a grand way.

Without even looking up from his game, Elroy said, "That poor girl. Not a lick of good sense."

"Yeah," said Willy back, moving one of his men on the board. "She ain't got the sense of Nicodemus. Crown me, please." He stamped the red checker hard against the board to let Elroy know that he was better at this game than he was.

They had been playing and having this same conversation for quite sometime. Years.

By now, Tammy Faye was out of sight, if not out of mind, and was gone. Gone for good. Though it would be several days or so before anybody noticed that Tammy Faye had disappeared.

Years back when everybody was young and vibrant and could get around quite freely without the help of a cane or a helping hand, the Lovejoys rode into the small town of Harper and moved into the old Bellamy mansion that sat off the road a good piece from town. And though the place was ugly—like mounds and mounds of ill-matched cemented bricks jigsawed together to form one of them spooky type castles that you see on a late night scary movie—the Lovejoys loved the place and decked the insides of the place with nothing but the finest: antique Victorian furniture, Oriental rugs, thick velvet draperies, soft white silk bed sheets and pillowcases, heavy cushiony quilts, nice wallpapers that had pictures of little boys and girls playing with puppies or huge red and pink roses that were in constant bloom. At least two hurricane lamps were in all of the rooms, and every niche and crevice that didn't have a tiny table full of crystal or porcelain odds-and-ends had a bookshelf, thick with first editions. Mr. Lovejoy was an avid reader of Greek and Roman philosophy. Mrs. Lovejoy loved poetry.

They were also Jehovah Witnesses, which made them some strange folks in Harper, being since everybody in town was born and bred and died Baptist or Presbyterian. Even for Witnesses, they were strange: didn't knock on anybody's door and had no intentions on knocking, either. Mr. Lovejoy didn't work in Harper, but each morning he left his home to drive the forty-miles to Memphis to do only God knows what. With such a fine house, most figured he had to be either a doctor or lawyer. The more creative folks in town decided he had to be some kind of gangster or part of some kind of mafia, since, after all, they believed people of those sorts all lived in Memphis. So, they all kept their distance for fear of angering Mr. Lovejoy and he put his boys on them.

Mrs. Lovejoy didn't work at all, didn't even go into town and never made a house call to any of the ladies' homes, though she was invited numerous of times when the family first arrived. She even hired a girl from the Harper High to do the groceries in town. After her first day at work, the poor girl went home to her mother and to about twelve of the women in town, who were waiting with tea cups in one hand and a brownie in the other to get the low-down on the insides of the Bellamy mansion.

The girl had nothing to tell. Honestly. She told them a young girl about her age named Tammy Faye greeted her at the door with a list of things to get from the groceries. That was it.

"You didn't even get a look at Mrs. Lovejoy? Or at least the insides of the place?" the mother inquired, holding her cup of tea in midair because all nosey people usually stop whatever they are doing to listen.

"No, mother," replied the girl. "Just Tammy Faye."

When time passes on like in any other town, big or small, people pass on. The Lovejoys died; first Mr. Lovejoy dropped dead of a heart attack while trimming hedges. All the women in Harper decided this would be the moment that they would get to see the inside of the Bellamy mansion, so most of them packed themselves in cars heading to Goldsmith's in Memphis to buy mourning dresses and lacey black funeral hats for the big event, except there wasn't an event. Not to mention big. Like thieves in the night, some relatives—their last name was Lovejoy, too, according to Mr. Holmes, the clerk that worked at the train depot—came into town on the evening train while everyone was sleeping and carried the remains back to Nashville, the place where the deceased Lovejoy was born. And that was that. Not a word. So, the only thing they could do was wait—wait for Mrs. Lovejoy to pass. Morbid, isn't it? But Mrs. Lovejoy continued, even out-living some of those who sat around waiting for her death. But when she died, way up in her eighties, again, the angels of death from Nashville came in on the late evening train and carried her back home to be next to her husband.

Then the mansion folded within itself more than ever.

Tammy Faye continued living in the house—now a plump middle-aged woman who rarely ventured outside, and only then to take a brisk walk through town when all other sensible people in the town were sleeping. A high school girl, always a different one every two to three years, one preceding the other through marriage or college, still came to the house to get the grocery list.

Then one day, no reason at all, Tammy Faye took to dancing at night in the streets. It was Mrs. Hollinsworth who first saw Tammy one night twirling around out on the front porch.

"She was just a-dancing," said Mrs. Hollinsworth to Mrs. Fletcher, who were both getting their hair clipped and teased at Mary's.

"What else she do?" asked Mrs. Fletcher, her whole head hanging almost completely out from under the dryer because you can't hear too well with one of those things going.

"Nothing, but just kept on down the street as late as it was, twirling and flapping her arms like she trying to get off the ground. Like one of them naked Las Vegas women."

"No!"

"Yes."

"I declare!"

It was a strange sight: a woman who had been a hermit for most of her life could now be seen on pale moonlit nights, dancing and twirling to music that no one heard except for her.

She had even started coming into town, which was newsworthy all by itself. But then she hauled Amy Pie, who at the time was the girl who did Tammy's shopping that year, up to the lunch counter at Luke's and ordered two hamburgers and two Coca-Colas. And when Luke Campbell told her that he wasn't serving neither one of them—one was black and the other just crazy. When he told them to get the hell out, Tammy Faye commenced to tearing up the place: throwing dishes and ashtrays and sugar bowls—running everybody out of the store. By the time Sheriff Taylor arrived she had already fried up the burgers and poured the Cokes. Since he had a soft spot for mentally disturbed folks, the sheriff arrested the other one. But besides that incident and other incidents like that, Tammy Faye stuck mostly to her dancing.

Tammy had taken to twirling down the street in the daytime now, telling everybody she met that she was going far away to be a dancer. The spectacle was watched by the whole town, though no one laughed except for little children. Everyone just breathed and shook their heads sorrowfully, like it was the worst tragedy since the time the school's boiler blew up and killed the janitor and they had no heat for a while.

Sometimes if the days were too hot for dance practice, she would stop up at the General Store for a soda pop, sitting quietly and watching Elroy and Willy play checkers.

"I'm going to be a dancer," she would start off, "just as soon as I get these steps right, I'm leaving this here place. I'm going to dance."

The men, though they heard every word she said, would not answer. They had stopped doing that about eight years back.

And after she had finished saying what she had to say, off the porch she would go, twirling and sometimes kicking up her legs, with a new wind, down the road, disappearing at the bend.

"Who in the hell is that crazy woman?" someone would ask, a visitor maybe, or someone who was not familiar with the Lovejoy family, who just so happened to be down at the town square taking care of legal business or whatever when the frumpy middle-aged woman twirled passed the courthouse.

"That's Tammy Faye Lovejoy. She's crazier than a loon. Her daddy died, then her mama passed away. Jehovah Witnesses. Just like that. And she ain't never been right since. Ain't never been out of the house, either, until about ten years ago."

"Wow, then bless her heart!"

There's not too much you can say about a person being crazy. God has special blessings for them, like when He watches over babies and fools. They are in His care.

Some of the local church ladies tried to get in touch with the Lovejoys in Nashville to tell them about their poor cousin or niece or whoever she was, but a letter promptly came back the next week stating that Tammy Faye was highly competent. It seemed as if the Nashville Lovejoys were only interested in their kin if they were dead.

So, Tammy Faye continued twirling down the streets, sometimes during the busiest times of the day so that if you were driving and thinking and got other things on your mind, you might have to swerve to the side to keep from hitting this lofty woman who was coming down Main Street.

The day the town realized that Tammy Faye disappeared into thin air was a summer Saturday morning, three days after she had made her last announcement to Willy and Elroy about going away to dance. Mrs. Hollinsworth called up Mrs. Fletcher one day to get a recipe for butter pound cake and just so happened to mention that she hadn't seen Tammy Faye twirling in a good while. So, Mrs. Fletcher called up Mrs. Colpepper, but Mrs. Colpepper told her that she saw Tammy Faye up there by the old sawmill last Monday morning. "Dancing in one of them teeny bopping skirts, I might add! I saw her myself."

"Well, that ain't true," said Mr. Colpepper, who just so happened to be up at the General Store not too long ago, last Wednesday to be exact, and heard Elroy and Willy talk about her dancing up on the porch while they were trying to finish off a serious game of checkers that very day and time where she was supposed to have been seen somewhere else.

Then other reports came back—the way news gets around in small towns—of Tammy Faye being spotted somewhere that she couldn't have possible been because of time or distance. It was just impossible. Whether it was true or not, everybody wanted to have spotted Tammy Faye somewhere. And just as soon as the reports had started, they stopped. She just disappeared. Just like that.

They thought maybe she had twirled over into the next county and would be home soon, but weeks began to turn into months and still no sign of Tammy Faye. Then the theories suddenly begin to pop up as to what could possibly have happened to Tammy Faye. It is an amazing thing, a town, that is, when it ceases being a group of people, but one single body—arms, legs, and a head—a perfect machine working within itself. The individuals are not thinkers or movers of their own bodies, but each contribute to the whole, acting together. This is what happened to Harper at the realization that Tammy Faye might be gone for good.

It was Judy Jackson, the Baptist minister's wife, who started the notion that Tammy Faye might be laid out dead up in that big house just waiting to stink up the whole town. So, when that idea got in the wind, all the men gathered together and hauled a tree—telephone pole size—and commenced to ramming in the front door of the Bellamy mansion. Not that they were really that concerned, but they just wanted something to ram and ransack. Of course, they found nothing. That is, they didn't find Tammy Faye. But some nice furniture out of the house seemed to have disappeared as quickly and mysteriously as its owners.

The other theory was that some wild drunken fraternity boys from Ole Miss must've found Tammy Faye twirling down one of them back roads and, since they are always laying low for some lascivious action between semesters, they decided to haul her off with them to their next party. Or maybe they were so drunk they didn't see her until their red convertible got right up on her and the last thing they saw was her bugged out eyes when the car mowed her down, so they hauled her off to some faraway woods over in the next county to be buried in a pasture under some hay. The wildest theory was by Pastor Jackson over at the Baptist church who preached that the Lord took Tammy Faye just like he did to that Enoch fellow in the bible. He said a fiery chariot lightening up the sky or whatever must've come to Harper and taken Tammy Faye away from us.

It was really a moving sermon—one person fainted and three spoke in tongues—and the whole congregation shook his hand and told Pastor Jackson how good his sermon was that Sunday.

James Pate was the one that asked Pastor Jackson how in the world could a chariot —not to mention a fiery chariot—come to Harper, Tennessee, without Willy and Elroy catching a glimpse of it. The pastor explained that it was only a figure of speech.

James rolled his eyes.

Yet, where was Tammy Faye?

There is only one tiny body of water in Harper. A stream so small you couldn't drown a gnat in it. So, she certainly didn't drown they decided. Everyone searched the woods, but nothing. Not one single clue. Some of the folks even walked the dusty road where she was probably last seen, at the bend, but there were no clues. They even hauled the blood-hounds out, who would be hot on a trail, but then suddenly, they would whine and bump heads and were usually ready to go back home.

It was James Pate again, the one who was a sophomore at Memphis State University who first said that Tammy Faye must've been cloned right before she disappeared.

"You mean she was turned into a bottle of perfume?" asked Willy, sitting on the general store's porch playing checkers with Elroy.

"Naw," said Jamie. "I said cloned, not cologne. She's been made into two people. One of her is here on earth and the other Tammy is probably standing on the Banks of Jordan, if you know what I mean. It's a natural scientific fact that explains stuff like this."

"Is that so?" asked Elroy, who was winning this particular game of checkers.

"Yes," answered Jamie, with a dingy smirk on his face, so you wouldn't know if he was lying through his damn teeth or laying down the truth. "You see, I hate to say it, but I do believe Tammy Faye is dead. Been dead for quite some time now. And what y'all been seeing is a couple of photoengraved copies of her real self. See?"

Of course, Elroy and Willy had stopped playing checkers. Forgotten all about the game.

"Whatever knocked her off must've done it so quickly and with such force 'till all of her didn't get a chance to leave. Different parts of her are still here."

"You mean to tell me we been seeing a haint all this time?" This was Willy, a cold chill running through his body so stiff until he couldn't concentrate on the checker game.

"Hell." This was Elroy, who was feeling the same chill on account that they both remembered her being just a few feet from them right on this porch just a few months ago.

The whole town continued their search for Tammy Faye for several more months, some even attempted to stop through Nashville on their way somewhere to do a little vacationing to see if she was living with the other Lovejoys. But the family knew nothing, or if they did, they did not speak of their missing relative.

Then slowly, Tammy Faye was forgotten. Years had passed and only the old people could remember a strange family named the Lovejoys that once lived in the Bellamy mansion. Sometimes the story was told about Tammy Faye and her love for twirling, always making up the part about what she did in that house all day, since no one knew. Maybe she just slept and danced all day. That was the fun part: making up what Tammy Faye did in that house, and there were several versions about that, too. But whenever it got to the part of whatever happened to her, the part where she made that twirl around that last bend, the storyteller, looking the listener square in the eye, would solemnly say quite honestly that

Tammy Faye Lovejoy just simply faded away.

Then it was one Sunday afternoon when Willy and Elroy were playing checkers up at the General and they had hauled a television out on the porch with them so they could watch the baseball game—Giants fans—throwing a few glances every once in a while, but they were mainly concentrating on the checker game.

But suddenly a commercial came on. It might have been the song. It might have been the dancing. But the two men stopped looking at the board to look at the screen. There was a woman dressed like a tube of toothpaste dancing across the screen testifying about how good Crest is for the teeth.

The men stared at the set. Then at each other. Then back at the set. Then at each other again.

"Is it?" asked Willy.

"I don't know."

They couldn't make out the face since it was painted white, and the whole head was partially covered with a hat that was shaped like a toothpaste cap. The way she danced and twirled brought back memories for the two men.

The lady dressed like a tube of toothpaste suddenly took a bow and she was gone. The baseball game was back.

"I'll be goddamned," said Elroy.

"It couldn't be," said Willy.

They kept playing the game, looking up every once in a while at the television.

THE CROQUET PLAYERS

There are only eleven of us—about sixty if you include the bottle of wines, beers, and vodka. Out on a lawn playing a game of croquet—whose lawn? Who knows? —and enjoying the weather: not too hot, not too cold. Perfect.

There are six lounging on blankets; there are five of us playing. There's music blasting: Jazz. The roaring 20s; except it's the 90s. In Memphis. Down by the edges of the Mississippi River in Harbor Town.

There is Frank, who is recording everything with his camera so the rest of us won't be able to lie about this event later.

There's Jerri, with a cigarette in one hand, shades on her face, and a martini in the other hand—in no particular order.

There's Mark—the stability of this whole evening, though as the afternoon progresses, we still have to fend for our own.

There are early afternoon joggers and walkers who see us out on the lawn playing. Most of them usually smile and wave as if they wanted to join in on the fun; others, with a baffled look, especially if they are an elderly couple, are either trying to decide if we are crazy or is it the 20s again.

We are all wearing white, except for Susan. It was Sandy's idea that we pretend to be characters out of *The Great Gatsby*. It goes over quite well.

So, here we are: a few hours later and we are getting slickered. We had forgotten the official rules of the game about an hour ago, and have created our own: just hit the balls hard enough, and whoever gets closer after three hits to the tall weeping willow without going past wins. Simple.

The ones who are not playing are cheering us on from the blankets they are lying on. Jerri—head cheerleader—is yelling for us to hit the ball. She is holding her third martini and is cussing. We turn and laugh at her when it's not our turn to play.

Everyone else is chattering: Susan is threatening Frank with a strong fist if he snaps another picture of her. Frank is laughing, but it's a nervous laugh as he backs away.

There is a little French woman named Michele here—we nicknamed her Fi-Fi—who had brought along a huge basket of food: baked salmon and roasted lamb and homemade breads. We cannot stop eating. She is one of the blanket dwellers, along with her daughter, Martini Girl—we forget her real name—who is sitting by the bar, which is actually a large cooler with several bottles of vermouth and vodka on the inside, and always a bottle of each sitting on top. Martini Girl is mixing the drinks as fast as we drink them.

Those who are playing are knocking the balls freely, not really caring too much about where they go, the sound of rising laughter floating in the warm summer Memphis air. These are the good times: not a care in the world and the liquor is steady flowing like the Mississippi that is rolling behind us as we enjoy ourselves near the banks.

It is Deborah who swings her mallet and sends the ball rocketing over in the thickets near the edges.

"My word, Deborah! Are you trying to send that ball to the moon, girl?"

We fall out laughing.

Deborah hikes up her ball gown and goes running off toward the edge of the river to the ball. She walks around over in the thick weeds searching for the lost ball. "Where in the hell did that damn ball go?" She staggers a little, but always catching herself just in time to move on further through the weeds.

"Oh, Deborah," yells Jerri from the blankets. "I

bet you there are snakes there just waiting to wrap their bodies around your little legs like a fine pair of socks. Please be careful."

"Just hurry up!" yell the other croquet players.

Deborah walks around the weeds some more, and then she stops. Suddenly, she starts screaming and running, forgetting to lift her dress from off the ground.

The blanket dwellers all jump up.

"You saw a snake didn't you?" asks Jerri. "I told you there were snakes." She takes a puff from her cigarette. "Y'all, didn't y'all hear me when I told Deborah that there were snakes down there. I could just feel it. My word."

Everybody is laughing.

"There's no damn snake down there. There's a dead man down there."

"What?"

Everybody starts rushing toward the thickets to take a look at the man that Deborah has found. Lying neatly over in the grass amongst the thick weeds is the body of a dead man. He is a young guy, about thirty or so. Clean cut and conservatively dressed in khakis and a Polo knit button-down. He is wearing a high school class ring. He does look as if he's sleeping, quite content and happy. There isn't a mark or blemish or anything on his face—as if he stepped out of the Sears, Roebuck catalog. It looks as though he had only recently died, for he hadn't even started to deteriorate, but looked like he had gotten tired and had simply fallen asleep besides the river.

The small group from the blanket joins those that are already peering over into the weeds. Faces all curled sourly, worried frowns slowly etched themselves across faces that ended with gaping mouths. Those who are holding martini glasses are holding them in midair, not moving, except for the olive in each glass that hasn't quite decided to settle down yet.

"Who do you suppose that is, Mark?" Jerri asks her husband.

"I don't know."

"My word," she replies

We continued to stare. Every once in a while someone would take a sip.

"I do declare! I've never seen a dead body before!" This is Susan, peering over the brush at the man. "Well, of course, I've seen dead folks before, but they are usually all dressed up and pretty and laying over in a casket. But nothing like this fellow all sprawled out like that. I can't bear to look at this." She continues her gaze.

"My word," Jerri repeats.

Sandy: "I reckon we ought to call the police."

"Oh, no, no, no," This is Deborah. "We can't possibly call the police in the state we are in."

"What state?"

"We've been drinking every since eleven this morning. How can we sensibly explain a murder?"

"How do you know he was murdered, Deborah?" asks Jerri.

"I don't know. Only a fool would choose to die on the banks of the Mississippi."

"That makes some sense there," says Susan sarcastically.

"It doesn't matter what state we are in," says Mark. "Our drinking is not on trial. There's a dead fellow here."

"Yeah, a dead fellow near *your* property," Deborah reminds him.

Frank, the photographer, snaps the young dead man's picture.

"My word!" shouts Jerri. "Oh, Mark, do you think they will haul us off to jail for murder? Now, Mark, you know I wouldn't kill a soul. "She takes another sip from the martini. "Now, if I were going to kill someone, it would have to be that JoAnn Churchill." She turns toward Susan and Deborah.

"She's just a demon in disguise is all she is."

The two other women shake their heads in agreement. They know JoAnn Churchill, also.

"Well, somebody needs to call the police. We just can't let this poor fellow just lie here for the rest of his—" Sandy suddenly realizes what he was about to say. "Well, for the rest of his death, rather."

Jerri laughs. "Sandy! That's so funny. Did y'all hear what Sandy just said?"

No one answers.

"Well, I ain't calling." This is Deborah. "Whenever I drink more than three martinis I got to confess everything. I'll call about this dead guy and the next thing I know I'll be telling them about all the unpaid parking tickets or the time I broke into Goldsmith's."

"What was that?" Everyone looks at Deborah as if they didn't know who she was.

"I mean, uh...if I had broken into Goldsmith one Christmas Eve to get some damn toy that I couldn't find anywhere else, I would be confessing it to the police right about now. That's what I meant." She nervously looks at everyone.

We look at her.

"I say one of us call the police and the rest of us just pack up and leave. No sense in all of us hanging out here like saloon cowboys and cowgirls."

"That's a good idea, Sandy," says Jerri. "You should stay."

Sandy laughs. "Why me?"

"Why, honey, it was your idea."

"Right, it was my idea. So, why am I being punished for having such bright ideas?"

"Well, to make you feel any better ah.... ahhhh...ahhh...what is your name? Sandy, yeah, that's right. Well, Sandy, I don't consider you all that bright." This is Susan. She decides that the martinis are clogging her memory with names and starts walking back up to the miniature bar for a glass of wine.

Finally, Fi-Fi decides that she had enough of this. "What is big deal here? I will call police. You Americans are insane totally." She is throwing up her hands, spilling her martini down her back, and grabbing another one from her daughter with the other hand. "I do not understand."

Deborah leans over and calms Fi-Fi down. "There, there, little French woman. Everything will be okay."

"I have a better idea," this is George, Susan's husband, who had been quiet the whole morning and afternoon. He and I are the only ones drinking beer, and since there is just a case left, we are secretly trying to drink fast so the other won't get as much.

Frank snaps George's picture.

"What's that?" we all want to know.

"Well," taking a sip from his almost empty can of beer, then looking up the hill toward the miniature bar to see if the last case was still there, and then looking over at me to see how much beer I had left in my full can. "Well, I say we play another game of croquet. Whoever comes in last has to call the police. The rest of us just leave."

"My word," this is Jerri again.

"George Simmons," says Susan, coming back from the bar with a glass of wine, "that is the craziest idea I've ever heard. What is wrong with you?"

Sandy, thinking about what George Simmons had said, pipes in, "I think it's a grand idea. Who's playing?"

"I'm sure in the hell not," says Deborah.

"You can just count me out, too."—Susan. "George Simmons, where in the world did you come up with such a crazy idea?"

George Simmons is laughing.

"HA!" says Mark. "This is pretty damn funny. Poor fellow, but this is pretty damn funny!"

True, I had never seen or heard anything like this.

I want to join in on the fun. Morbid, I know, but how often does a person get to participate in something like this?

"I'm in," I say. "Martini Girl, fill me up again!"

So, there are seven of us playing a game of croquet: Mark, Sandy, George Simmons, Frank, Martini Girl, and me. The rules are changed slightly: whoever is farther away from the weeping willow has to call the police to report a death.

Jerri looks up into the sky, "Jesus? Do you see what is happening here? Your children have lost their minds." She shakes her head and takes another sip from a fresh martini.

The game is on! George Simmons is first since he says it is his idea, then Mark, Sandy, Martini Girl, then me and finally Frank. All of us hit about the same during the first and second rounds of the game—nowhere.

During the last shot of the first round, Sandy staggers over to take his turn and accidentally kicks the ball forward with his foot.

"Say, you dirty bastard," Mark says. "We saw you."

"I didn't mean to do that."

"The hell you didn't." Mark is waving his mallet like he is going to use it on Sandy's head.

"All right. All right." Sandy picks up the ball and brings it back even further from its original position. "Are you satisfied now?"

"Hell yeah."

The rest of us laugh. Mark and Sandy eye each other for the rest of the game.

Martini Girl is the first to knock her ball to some distance. Just a few feet, but still nowhere near the weeping willow.

"She's going to whip our asses," says George Simmons.

Martini Girl giggles. It is only fitting that she should be winning. She has had the least amount to drink.

I am as drunk as the other men. I am in second place behind Martini Girl, so I am certain that I wouldn't be calling the police. I am in a good mood. Martini Girl and I are in the clear. The real game is between Mark, Sandy and George Simmons.

"What in the hell is going on down there?" asks Jerri.

"Are you winning, George Simmons?" This is Susan. "Cause you're too drunk to be calling any police. Just leave good deeds to sober folks."

George Simmons looks up the hill, and throws his hands at his wife: hush woman, his hands say.

"All right now, George Simmons," she warns. "Don't make me come down there."

We laugh.

When Sandy's turn comes—again he kicks the ball.

"All right, dirty bastard!" This is Mark, raising his mallet and holding it right in Sandy's face. "Do you want me to use this?"

The blanket dwellers stretch out completely and howl with laughter, grabbing their stomachs.

"Dear Jesus, I'm going to be sick!" yells Jerri.

The two men are cussing at each other: Mark calling Sandy a cheating sonofabitch, Sandy calling Mark a blind bastard. And if they are not loud enough, George Simmons is screaming for both of them to shut the hell up. He is being louder than the both of them put together. Martini Girl, Frank and I, as well as the blanket dwellers are steady howling up a storm.

"I do believe I'm about to pee in my pants," declares Deborah, trying her best to catch her breath.

"Oh, my!" says Fi-Fi, thowing a hand over her mouth in disbelief.

"Jesus, please help Deborah and her bladder," prays Jerri. She's serious about this prayer.

"Either you quit kicking the ball, or I'm going to

start swinging this mallet like Willie Mays," threat-ens Mark.

Sandy knows Mark means business. Again, he picks up the ball and brings it back further from where it should have been.

"There!" says Sandy, glaring at Mark.

"There my ass!" says Mark. "Do it again and that ball won't be the only thing that will be kicked from here to Georgia."

Everybody is falling out again.

The game starts back. It is Martini Girl's turn. With her first martini in her hand, she single hand-edly knocks her ball through the final loop and it shoots passed the weeping willow.

Everybody cheers.

Martini Girl curtseys and then walks up to the miniature bar and commences to making more martinis for everyone.

Just then, a squad car is slowing pulling up be-sides the street. It is Fi-Fi that first notices the police car. "The Fuzzy!" she screams and points.

Everyone looks up the hill toward the street.

"That's 'the fuzz", Deborah corrects Fi-Fi, patting her on the hand.

"The fuzz," says Fi-Fi. "Fuzz or fuzzy. He is here to"—she stops for a second or two—"he is here to whip names and take asses."

Deborah shakes her head.

The officer parks the car and gets out. He is quite tall, well over six feet, six-three, six four maybe. A young black guy who looks to be no more than thirty years, if that old.

"Well, my my my my," says Deborah, grabbing her purse to look for her make-up kit.

Those of us that are playing stop what we are doing and to see what is going on, walking up the hill to be with the blanket dwellers. We are all confused.

The officer comes into the yard, smiling, taking a quick look at the empty bottles of vodka and vermouth, and then giving us all a quick scrutiny. "How y'all doing today?" asking as if he already knew, but just wanted to see what the answers would be.

"We're doing just fine, honey," answers Deborah.

He smiles at Deborah. "Well, guys, I hate to be the bearer of bad news, but someone called and reported some disturbance. Said you are all too loud."

All of us breathe a sigh of relief.

"That's a relief," says Deborah, patting the sweat from her forehead. "We thought you were out here because—"

Jerri smacks Deborah on the shoulder.

"Well, we will try to tone it down, officer. We

didn't realize we were so loud." This is Mark. "I guess we were really into this game." He laughs nervously.

"Yeah," says Sandy.

I nod my head with the rest of them.

"Do you play croquet?" Sandy asks the officer.

"No, never played before," he answers.

"Well, come on and we'll show you."

The officer smiles. "No, no thank you. I think I will pass this time."

We all yell for the officer to go down the hill and play for at least five minutes. He decides to go, mainly to shut us up.

"Deborah? Is he not a stud?" Jerri asks Deborah when the officer has walked off.

"I'm having hot flashes," Deborah answers.

"How big are his feet, Deborah? Did you get a chance to look at them?"

"Damn, I forgot to look."

"Well, go on down that hill, girl, and check his feet out."

Deborah gets up, hikes up her ball gown and trots down the hill where the others are teaching the officer to play the game.

"Why are y'all so concerned about this fellow's feet?" asks Susan, frowning up, not really sure what is going on.

"Well, Susan, darling, " says Jerri, "bless your heart, honey, you know what they say about men with big feet." She fans herself some more.

"Oh, shit," laughs Susan. "That is not true, cause George Simmons got—"

"Oh, Jerri!" This is Deborah trotting back up the hill toward the blanket dwellers. "He's wearing a good size thirteen or fourteen shoe!"

"My word," says Jerri as she falls back onto the blanket as if exhausted. She starts to fan herself with one of the paper fans that she has out here with her. "Now, Deborah, tell me, what in the world would you do with a man with feet that big?"

The women fall out laughing again.

We forget about the poor dead fellow lying in the thickets. I suck my can of beer down. I think the players down the hill have forgotten also.

"My word!" says Jerri. "We forgot about that poor dead fellow!"

Susan, Deborah and Fi-Fi throw their hands over their mouths in horror and stare at one another.

Jerri starts to fan herself once again.

I suck down the last amount of beer in my bottle and grabbed another one.

Finally, the officer comes back from the banks. "I

really must go. I am working you know," he tells us, smiling.

"Okay, bye," the blanket dwellers immediately tell him.

Frank snaps the officer's picture.

The officer waves, gets in his car and pulls off.

"My word!" Jerri says. "That was close. Jesus in heaven."

Everyone sighs.

"Sandy, darling," asks Susan, "what in the hell were you thinking inviting him down there to play?"

Sandy laughs. "I forgot all about that dead fellow."

"HA!" exclaims Mark.

"My word."

The men go back to their game. Mark and Sandy are steadily cussing each other. They are trying to keep their voices down, but it's hard to do.

The sun is beginning to set on the edges of the river. It has been a nice day.

~~~~~

Later this evening, Sandy was the one that lost in the game of croquet. We just simply packed up: the miniature bar, the plates of breads and other foods, the empty bottles of wines and beers, dirty napkins.

"I wish I knew more about John," said Jerri.

"Who is John?"

"The poor dead fellow"

"How do you know his name is John?" we wanted to know.

"I don't know. He looks like a John. Don't you think? I would hate to die and the first people to see me dead are a bunch of people who don't know a thing about me. I think that's terribly sad."

We stood there in the yard for a moment—silent and thoughtful. Terribly sad.

We finished packing up our things and started walking to the cars. No one was talking.

Sandy was all that was left behind. He was on a cellular phone dialing the number for the police.

"I say we go downtown and have a drink in poor John's honor," said Mark.

"I do believe that's a grand idea, Mark!"

We decided to go on Beale and have a few more drinks and hold a memorial service for John.

"Meet us down on Beale somewhere," Mark yelled to Sandy.

Sandy nodded his head.

As we turned the bend to head out, we passed the same officer that we had spoken with earlier. I wondered if the police would have to speak to all of us eventually. I wondered if we would be suspects. It might have been important to worry about this, but right now, we had to make sure John will be okay.

Jerome Wilson

A TREE FOR CHRISTMAS

We sitting around watching TV and eating pop-corn when we see Mrs. Walters walking past the big picture window.

"Turn the TV off!" Mama say and Maggie crawl—we are already on the floor watching *The Dukes of Hazzard*—over to the TV and click the knob.

Then the three of us—that's me, mama and my sister, Maggie—get quiet when Mrs. Walters ring the doorbell. She wait. We wait.

I poke Maggie in her side and she squirm and poot and start giggling. Then Mama point her finger at both of us to let us know she ain't up for our foolishness.

She ring it again. She wait. We wait. Then she ring it again. After awhile, we hear her shuffle off the porch and tip back across next door to her house.

"Lord Jesus, why can't that old woman quit bothering us?" Mama ask, clicking the TV back on, just in time to hear Bo and Luke tearing through the

Georgia back roads in their General Lee. "Damn."

Me and Maggie look at each other and fall out laughing. We always laughing when we hear Mama cussing on account she hardly ever cuss.

Mrs. Walters is the old white lady that lives by herself next door to us on Catherine Street. She is always knocking on our door and coming in and sitting and talking to Mama while Mama is trying to cook and clean or both. Sometimes Mrs. Walters don't talk, but just sit in the den with us. Sometimes she goes to sleep and this scares me and Maggie to death on account Mrs. Walters is real old and we thinking she is going to die one day in the chair she likes sitting while we're all watching *The Muppet Show*.

Sometimes she bring us food to eat, but Mama make us dump it in the garbage can. If she ask us how we like the muffins that she made for us, we suppose to say that they were good. Mama said that she ain't clean on account she got wet snuff at both corners of her mouth and she blows her nose with her hands and wipe the snot on her dress. Me and Maggie see her do that one time and we just fall out laughing. We are always falling out laughing over something.

Mama say that we need to stop giggling so much

or folks are going to think that we ain't got good sense. We fall out laughing even harder when she say that.

So now we in the den—me and Maggie and Mrs. Walters—and we watching *Frosty the Snowman*. Mama is running around the house trying to get everything cleaned up and situated because the day after tomorrow will be Christmas Eve. Aunt Dorothy and Uncle Curtis are coming over for dinner so she don't have time to sit and chat with Mrs. Walters, who worked her way in the house when she caught Mama outside emptying the garbage can.

So when we see Mrs. Walters coming through the back door with Mama, me and Maggie look at each other and we are about to laugh on account we figure Mrs. Walters must've caught Mama at the garbage cans outside—but we don't laugh cause Mama is looking at us like if she hear one sniggle from us she's going to slap both our faces. So we giggling inside ourselves.

Mama tell Mrs. Walters that she can't talk right now cause she busy cleaning, which is the same as saying: "GO HOME!", but that is no never mind because Mrs. Walters don't catch hints and is always sitting around with me and Maggie watching TV and going to sleep.

"What Santa Claus is gonna bring you?" she asking both of us.

Maggie tell her that she is getting a See'n' Say and a Lite-Brite and some clothes and a doll and this and that.

I'm going to tell her about my new clothes I'm getting and another Evel Kneivel action figure because Daddy accidentally ran over the one I got last year for Christmas.

But before I can tell her what I'm getting Mrs. Walters is sleeping again—head all the way back, with her mouth hanging like all the other times except this time we don't hear no snoring and snorting and carrying on like she is always doing. She is too quiet. Too still. At first we don't pay it no mind, but keep on watching TV, holding our breaths when the magic man take his hat back from Frosty even though we've seen this a ton of times.

I don't know who catch the idea first—me or Maggie—but we suddenly see that Mrs. Walters ain't making no noise.

"She ain't snoring, " say Maggie.

"I know," I say back.

We look at her for a long time.

Me and Maggie looking at each other cause we don't know what else to do. We sit for a while waiting for her to wake up like she always doing, but she ain't moved yet.

"Is she dead?" Maggie ask me.

"I don't know." I try looking at her stomach to see if it's going up and down, but I don't see nothing. I declare I don't.

We scoot a little closer—but not too close—so maybe we can hear her breathing or something. But we don't hear nothing.

"Maggie, go up and put your ear to her mouth."

"Who?"

"You."

"No!"

"Go on. Ain't nothing going to happen."

"I know it ain't 'cause I ain't going."

So we steady sit there on the floor some more trying to figure out what to do. We don't want to go get Mama, because if she ain't dead then Mama will get mad at us for bothering her while she's cooking and carrying on. And if she is dead then Mama will still be mad on account she got to deal with getting an old dead woman out our den while she got three cakes and an egg custard going in the oven.

So we just steady wait. We even look at TV some more, but steady cutting our eyes over at Mrs. Walters.

After awhile Maggie nudge me to make me go put my ear up to Mrs. Walters who is still in the chair and ain't move one bit.

I get off the floor and tip. I look back at Maggie and she is throwing her hand over her mouth to keep from laughing. I whisper to her to shut up. I keep tipping. Now I'm standing so close to Mrs. Walters now that I can smell her. She smell like oldness and pee. She is quiet. I don't think I have ever been this close to her. Her face is pasty like clown make-up. She got snuff stains at the corner of her mouth and a couple of stains around the front of her dress.

I swallow hard. I decide to put my hand up to her nose and see if I feel any heat blow on me. I think I do, but I'm not sure. I turn around and look back at Maggie and she is grabbing her ear to tell me to listen to her mouth. I turn back and look at Mrs. Walters who still ain't move one single inch. I swallow again and get ready to bend over to put my ear up to her mouth.

Suddenly somebody grab me at the back of my collar like a mama cat grabbing her kittens and start shaking me.

"Boy, what in the world are you doing?" Mama trying her best to whisper but it's still loud.

""I...we...thought..."

"Leave that woman alone! What were you doing?"

"We thought...."

"Shut up! What were you doing?"

"We thought she was ..."

"Didn't I tell you to shut up? Get over there and sit down with your sister and leave that woman alone!"

I go sit down next to Maggie. She is looking scared too because Mama is all upset and fussing. She keep on fussing even when she walking out of the den to go see about the cakes and the custard in the oven.

Me and Maggie look at each other for a long time and then we just bust out laughing. Not the quiet laughing like we usually do when we don't want anybody to know we laughing at them. We ain't howling either, but we ain't keeping it to ourselves.

This make Mrs. Walter wake up, and she wake up laughing trying to help us laugh at Frosty even though *Frosty the Snowman* been gone off the TV a long time ago. *Rudolph, the Red-Nosed Reindeer* is on now.

"Y'all laughing at Frosty?" she asking, talking baby talk to us like we some retarded babies. "You like that Frosty? What that Frosty doing? You like that Frosty?"

I say, "Yes, ma'am," because Maggie is steady giggling.

"Yeah, that Frosty is funny." Then she fall back to sleep.

I cut my eyes at Maggie, and we laugh some more.

~~~~~

Today is Christmas Eve. Me and Maggie got to get baths and have ourselves ready for dinner tonight. When I'm putting on my clothes and watching the TV at the same time, I see Mrs. Walters walking passed the picture window and she's carrying a tiny little Christmas tree.

She ring the doorbell. I'm not sure what to do. I want to answer the door because she is toting a Christmas tree, but I don't think Mama and daddy want to talk to Mrs. Walters today. So I just stand there looking at the door.

Daddy come out of the bedroom and say, "Who at the door?"

I whisper, "Mrs. Walters."

"Don't you answer that door!" he say, and he not even whispering.

So we both are standing there looking at the door and listening to her ring. Then Maggie come running out cause she's happy to see Aunt Dorothy, but by the way we're standing around and looking at the door, she know it's Mrs. Walters.

"Will somebody get the door!" Mama yelling from the kitchen.

"Shhhh!" say Daddy even though he ain't whispering when he says it.

We all just looking at the door. Finally, she leave, and the first thing I do is peep out the window at her to see if she is toting the tree back with her. She ain't. I smile. I tell Maggie she left us a tree.

Daddy go back in the bedroom to sleep.

When we think she is back in her own house, me and Maggie open up the front door. Sure enough, there is this tiny little tree sitting on the porch.

"Wow!" say Maggie, like the tree just spoke to her.

The tree is decorated with tiny little ornaments and little bells on just about every little branch. It even got little baby Christmas lights.

"Wow," Maggie say again.

We get it and bring it in the house and set it on the coffee table. Me and Maggie don't say nothing but just sit and stare at it. It got a button for the lights and when I press it Maggie say "Wow" again for the third time because the tree is lighting up.

There is a card attached to the tree, "Merry Xmas,

Maggie and Sonny Buck."

Me and Maggie sit and watch the tree for a long time.

Later on Aunt Dorothy and Uncle Curtis are over here for dinner. She is my Mama sister. She always taking us and riding us on her lap. Now she just ride Maggie because she say I'm getting to be a big boy now and I'm liable to break her legs in half. She is always telling me to let Uncle Curtis ride me, but I don't ask him nothing 'cause he looks foolish. Always sitting around smiling to hisself when nothing ain't funny—real nervous acting like he just robbed a bank and the word ain't got out yet. Mama says that he is a bona fide cheapskate and ain't got the sense of Nicodemus. Wouldn't take Aunt Dorothy to McDonald's if her life depended on it.

I ask Mama who is Nicodemus, but she tell me to stop asking grown folks questions.

So we all eating dinner. Me and Maggie, looking at each other, trying to keep from laughing on account Uncle Curtis is at the table eating up everything and not even thinking about there's other folks at the table, not to mention he ain't come up for breath from the table for hours it seem like. Then Mama giving me and Maggie that look that said that we better act right at this table, which of course make us want to laugh even harder.

When we on our second plate, Uncle Curtis is on his fourth or fifth and Mama looking like she want to tell him to stop and go home somewhere. But she steady say nothing, just cut her eyes at Daddy and he cut his back at her like he want to say: "I don't know, either."

After awhile we all full and just sit around picking our teeth.

Pretty soon Uncle Curtis get up from the table and say that he need to go visit his folks. I look at Mama, and Mama and Aunt Dorothy look at each other on account Uncle Curtis is always saying he going out to Olive Branch to visit his folks, even though everybody in the world know he go see this shaky dress lady that sell car parts for Autozone on the other side of town who takes all of his money and don't even leave him change in his pockets to buy himself a Coca-Cola. That's what I heard Mama and Aunt Dorothy talking about one day over the phone.

"Don't be gone too long now. I want to get a tree."

He don't answer.

Nobody say a word when he's walking out the door.

I wonder why don't Aunt Dorothy ever shoot at him being since she totes a gun even though she can't see good, which is why Mama is always putting away Aunt Dorothy's coat and purse, and not me or Maggie on account Mama think the pistol might go off and shoot one of us. One time I ask Mama why don't Aunt Dorothy shoot him and get it over with. She slap my face and told me to quit asking grown folks questions.

The doorbell ringing again and we see it's Mrs. Walters.

Daddy get up and go in the back room to sleep. He is always sleeping when he ain't working.

"Lord Jesus Almighty in the sweet heavenly blue skies above!" say Mama.

Aunt Dorothy fall out laughing. "Mattie, you crazy!"

Then Mama start laughing.

"Girl, she still alive? I don't believe it."

"Course she still alive. You hear that bell ringing don't you? Sonny Buck, open that door before that old woman bust my eardrums to pieces."

Aunt Dorothy holler some more. Both of them.

I open the door and Mrs. Walters is smiling. "Did Sonny Buck and Maggie get old Mrs. Walter's Christmas present?"

I smile. "Yes ma'am. Thank you." I step back cause she is already inviting herself inside for a sit-down.

"Come on in, Mrs. Walters, and have a sit-down," say Mama. "You know my sister, Dorothy?"

"I do believe I will. Yes, I met her before, " she say, even though she ain't never seen Aunt Dorothy before, trying her best to get through the door without falling on account she wearing heels like she's going to church but she ain't. She is always wearing heels and church dresses and necklaces and rings like she's going off somewhere. But she don't go nowhere but to her front porch, to the mailbox, or over to our house. Mama say that all her jewelry is real.

She sit down in her favorite chair and tell me to come to her. "You know, my daddy bought me that tree when I was a little girl. That thing is old. It's been in my attic for years. I didn't want anything to happen to it, you know. And when my nephew came by the other day, I told him to bring that tree down 'cause I wanted to give it to my two children next door. Where is Maggie?"

"She sleep," I say.

"Okay," she say. She reach down in her dress pocket and pull out two dollars. "Okay, you take one and give your sister one when she wakes up."

"Yes, ma'am," I say. And before I can say "thank

you" my Mama ask me, "What are you suppose to say, Sonny Buck?"

"Thank you," I say.

"That's right. You know I taught you better than that."

"You welcome, baby. Now give old Mrs. Walters a hug." She throw out her arms.

I hug her, even though I don't want to because she stinks, but I do because I don't want to make her sad. She smells like snuff.

I go back to watching TV.

Mrs. Walters fall asleep.

Mama and Aunt Dorothy look at each other like they want to laugh, but they just turn and watch TV, too. Pretty soon they sleep, too. We all sleep.

After a while Mrs. Walter wake up and say, "Well, let me go on. My nephew is coming by to take me to dinner with David and Nancy."

She is always naming folks we don't know like we know them; she is telling us some bad news about folks that we don't even know or never heard of, but she tell it like we have known them for years and years. "Y'all take it easy."

"Bye, Mrs. Walters," we all say.

She ease on down the steps and back across the yard to her own house.

"Where her coat at?" The first thing Aunt Doro-thy ask when I close the door.

"I don't know, child," say Mama.

"Bless her heart."

"Poor lonesome soul," say Mama.

"Good God, she was funkier than a damned go-rilla!"

"I know that's right!" say Mama.

Mama and Aunt Dorothy fall out laughing again.

Pretty soon we hear Uncle Curtis coming up the street on account his Nova is always backfiring and missing. He come inside and ask everybody how they doing, even though it's just me and Mama and Aunt Dorothy sitting here in the den. He is sniffing at the air because Mrs. Walters ain't too long ago left.

"Fine," we all say.

"Don't sit down," Aunt Dorothy say. "We need to go now. I want to get a tree."

He laugh like it was the funniest thing he had ever heard in his life. "What you need a tree for? It's Christmas Eve already. You get a tree and put it up tonight, you got to put it away the next day."

"I don't care! You promised me a Christmas tree. You cheap bastard—Oh!" She look over at me.

"Pardon your auntie's French, baby."

We all laugh.

By this time Daddy come out to see what all the hollering is all about and walk right in the middle of Aunt Dorothy calling Uncle Curtis everything except for a child of God.

"What's all this racket here?"

"Trying to get this nigger to get me a tree."

We all fall out laughing again.

"Dorothy, you crazy!" Mama say, catching her stomach at the same time because laughing on a full stomach don't feel good.

"Well, why don't you take that one," Daddy say.

I suddenly don't feel good. Mainly, my stomach, but my face ain't feeling so good either. I suddenly feel hot like somebody just slapped me. Everybody just look at the tree that is sitting on the coffee table.

"Naw," Aunt Dorothy say. "That's Sonny Buck's."

"Awe, he don't need it. He's too big for a tree like this," say Mama.

I look at Mama to see if she's making a joke at me. But I don't think she is joking. Now I really feel sick.

"No!" I say.

"Shut up, boy," Daddy say.

I suddenly feel like crying because now I know they are not joking with me.

"Naw, Mattie. I ain't going to take this boy's tree. He's going to buy me one tonight," Aunt Dorothy darting her head at Uncle Curtis's direction.

"Why don't you take the tree?" Uncle Curtis say. "It's free."

"Girl, take that tree!" Mama say. "Sonny Buck don't need it, I tell you. Take it."

"Take the tree," say Daddy again and I look at him when he walk over and get the tree off the coffee table.

"No!" I say, and I try to take it from him. "It's mine!"

Daddy set the tree down and before I know it he grab me by my collar and say, "Don't you ever snatch nothing out of my hand!" And after he finish shaking me some more he say, "Go to bed!"

I run to my room and I cry.

I hear them talking in the den, fussing about that tree but I don't care what they are saying. Then I hear them leave and Mama and Daddy saying their good-byes.

I still cry.

After a while Daddy come in my room with his belt in his hand and he grab me straight off the bed by the back of my pants and whip me until he is breathing too hard to keep whipping. Then Maggie come out of her room, rubbing her eyes and wanting to know what is happening.

"Go back to bed, Maggie." He drop me back in my bed.

"If Mrs. Walters ask about that tree y'all tell her that it's in the attic for safe keeping," say Mama.

"Why the tree in the attic?" Maggie ask.

"Go to bed," Mama and Daddy say to her, even though she is looking mighty confused and wanting to know what is happening.

"Why the tree in the attic?" she still want to know.

"Didn't I tell you to go to bed?"

Slowly, Maggie go back to her room, but she is still talking trying to figure out what is going on and they steady telling her to go to bed.

Finally, I don't hear none of them talking now because I'm thinking about tomorrow being Christmas. I stop my crying and keep thinking about that until I fall asleep.

Bound for
the Promised Land

I'm leaving Memphis! Been packing my things ever since day before yesterday morning, and I'll be leaving this place just as soon as my niece come and get me. Mrs. Walters been over here yesterday helping me get my stuff together. She's really nice like that. It ain't like I hate Memphis or anything like that, though God knows I got a heap of reasons to despise it. But I try to keep hate out my heart, and bricks off my head and bullets out my window-panes. Which is one of the main reasons I'm leaving while I'm still alive and the getting is still good. The shooting can get so bad around here some nights, you'd swear it was Dodge City. You might think I might go out there and tell them to cut out all that racket being since I know all who's shooting because I used to let them play jumpfrog in my front yard and gave them candy money and fed some of them dinner when their mamas couldn't be found. But I don't go nowhere to tell nobody to stop nothing.

That's why I'm going to live with my niece, since

she got an extra bedroom and said I could come and stay with her and Big Eddie and Eddie, Jr. anytime I want to because she's real nice like that. Even though I don't like Big Eddie too well. He always smell like smoke and liquor and always know everything about anything you throw out at the dinner table. Hell, I'm passed seventy and I know I don't know everything in the entire world; and him being only thirty-five, I know he ain't doing nothing but lying. So, most times, when he get on a roll and try explaining to me the scientific reason why snakes shed their skin, or when he try to relate to me the proper way to put a damn bait on a fishing hook, I just nod my head and tell him I understand like the retarded fool he think I am—which I ain't, of course—and the genius he think he is—which, of course, he ain't. But I don't mind playing these charades with this fool because he's my niece's husband and she loves him and I love her and Eddie, Jr. So, damn Big Eddie.

Rose, my niece, is my little brother John-John's daughter. The only daughter he ever had. He's dead and gone now, bless his heart, but he left a fine daughter.

I remember when she just got out of high school, she called me and Myrtle up and said, "Uncle Lester? Can I move to Memphis and stay with you and Aunt Myrtle while I go to school?" That was when they were just starting to let black folks in at Memphis State, you know. Of course, I said yes, and so did Myrtle, because we wasn't ones to slow young folks down who was trying to get a piece of education. Plus, me and Myrtle never had any children to spoil to death. So, we were glad for her to come. She stayed with us a little over four years. Myrtle loved her to death. I did, too. Still do. We hated it when she left. But folks got to go on with their lives, you know.

She told us, "Uncle Lester, Aunt Myrtle, I appreciate everything, everything y'all done for me."

That made us feel so good. Most folks nowadays wouldn't thank you for saving their lives. Some folks just ain't grateful.

And when Myrtle passed away twelve years ago, Rose was right there with me. She wanted me to move in with her right then, but I told her no. I could take care of myself. And besides, she had just married Big Eddie, which was a mistake from the word go—I didn't tell her this—and she didn't need her old uncle in the way of a new marriage, even though it was bound for hell real soon anyway. Of course, I didn't tell her that, either.

"But Uncle Lester, we got an extra bedroom. Eddie won't mind. And you know Eddie, Jr. loves you to death."

To be honest with you, it sure did sound tempting. I knew Big Eddie wouldn't have cared; as much as he started to stay out drinking, it would've been about two years before he realized I was living there. He's real dumb like that.

And I love Eddie, Jr. and he loves me. When I finally made it out there to see him after he was born he was already crawling. And when he saw me he just smiled and crawled right up into my lap like he knew me all along. And he even cried when I had to leave! He looks just like his mama. A little like his daddy. Poor thing.

He sent me a picture one time. It was a picture of him graduating out of kindergarten. He didn't have a lick of teeth in his head—you ought to see this—and there he was, just smiling up a storm. I hollered! I put some clothes on and went next door to Mrs. Walters and showed her the picture.

"Mrs. Walters, look at this picture my great-nephew done sent me. Ain't this something?"

I thought she was going to die laughing. Both of us laughed so hard we couldn't do nothing for the rest of the day but sit around and sip on coffee.

So, you see, it wouldn't have been a problem for me to move out there with my niece. I just wanted to be on my own at the time.

It wasn't that I was happy Myrtle was gone. Lord knows she suffered enough. And if it wasn't for my family and friends, I probably would've lost my mind. And even now, I sometimes forget and put another plate down at the dinner table, and I sometimes holler her name and ask her has she seen my socks. Stuff like that. I guess that's my mind slipping. But sometimes I do see Myrtle walking around the house. Most times she just waves and keep on doing what she's doing, which is always busy walking into the next room. It don't matter what room I'm in. If I'm in the bedroom, she's waving at me and heading toward the kitchen. If I'm in the kitchen, she's on her way to the living room. Even when she was alive I couldn't keep up with that woman. I ain't told a soul about Myrtle still being here with me. Folks always want to cart you off somewhere whenever you tell them something they can't understand—or don't want to understand. Especially when you old. Second, she ain't hurting nobody, and I'm scared if I tell somebody she might stop visiting me, and I want to keep Myrtle in any form I can have her.

So not wanting to stay with nobody didn't have a

thing to do with me hating my marriage with Myrtle. That is to say, I didn't hate my marriage. I just wanted my niece to know that Lester Pruitt could take care of himself. And I've done a pretty good job, thank you very much.

I'm not saying I don't need nobody's help. If it wasn't for Rose coming to Memphis after Myrtle's death to help me sort things out, I don't know what I would've done. And Rose sure did take care of me when I had my stroke about three years ago. I really appreciated that. I love Rose. She's nice like that.

You know, she even calls me every week. She always saying something like, "Uncle Lester? You feeling okay today?"

"Just fine, Rose. How you?"

"I'm doing fine. You eating okay?"

"Yes. How's Eddie, Jr.?"

"He's okay. Made the honor roll. You're not hurting anywhere are you, Uncle Lester?"

"No," I always say, even if I'm really in pain. Ain't no need in worrying herself when she already got a family to worry with. She's real kind like that.

Right before she gets off the phone she saying how much it hurts her heart to see me living with no friends and no one to look after me.

But I got friends, I tell her. There's Mrs. Walters

living next door. Been living next door even before I got here. And that's almost thirty-five years. That's when it was safe to sit on your porch and not worry about bullets meeting you at the steps. Ha! Ha! The reason I mentioned bullets when discussing Mrs. Walters is because the most awfullest thing happened to her about a year ago.

One night them kids got to shooting up the street like cowboys. As usual, I hauled my ashes down on the floor next to my bed. I was on the floor a good whole five minutes when I heard somebody hollering, "You fools stop all that shooting!"

It was Mrs. Walters. That crazy woman had walked out on the porch trying to make them bastards stop. She even called them by their names because they used to play on her front porch and she used to give them money and candy when they were little. Me and Myrtle used to do the same thing, but you already know where I was when them guns got to banging. Anyway, the next thing you know, a bullet come whizzing her way. She damn near tore the hinges off the door trying to get back inside. She walks with a cane, but she forgot it that night. Poor thing. No use in calling the authorities. You and I both know how dumb black folks can get when the police roll around.

She came over the next morning and told me what had happened. "Mr. Pruitt," she said, and you can't help but to smile at this woman because she brings everything to life. That's Mrs. Walters for you. She can twist any tragic death scene into a one-woman comedy skit good enough to be put on anybody's stage. "Those kids are crazy! Just plain crazy! You know, one of them bullets went straight through my house and put a hole in the jug of milk I had sitting out on the table. Lord, I spent the rest of the night soaking up milk and wrestling with eight hungry cats! Ain't that awful?"

I thought I was going to bust a gut I laughed so hard. That's the way Mrs. Walters is. Just as funny. Like I said, she's been living in the neighborhood for years. That's back when this neighborhood—or this street, at least—had nice yards and gardens and everybody looked out for one another and your child play outside all day and not worry about somebody snatching them. Me and Myrtle moved here in the early sixties and it was still nice. Nice folks, too. This was the only place middle- and upper-class blacks could live, you know. Doctors and lawyers and school teachers. Nice folks, too. Even a couple of politicians. They were nice, too.

But I said all that to say this: Mrs. Walters is my

friend. She used to be a school teacher. Just like my Myrtle. Mrs. Walters been retired for years now. Mr. Walters recently died about five years ago. Dropped dead of a heart attack right there in the front yard. I saw it, too. He worked as a garbage man. Lord, that man could tell you some stories about when King came to town. I loved to hear him talk. I worked as a construction worker, so we rode the bus together on some days. Bless his heart. I miss that fellow. Ain't that something? But Mrs. Walters, she's been carrying on though. She gets around okay on her cane. Sometimes she calls on me to help her do things she can't handle. So between the two of us—her on her cane, and me, slightly paralyzed on my left side because of my stroke about three years ago—we can usually change that light bulb or move the furniture out from the wall so she can sweep back there. It might take us a long time, but we get the job done!

My other friend is the mail lady. She's the cutest little thing you ever want to lay your eyes on. You ought to see her. Lord Jesus, she got dimples, too! Tiffany Clark. That's her name. Tiffany. Tiffany. Ain't that a pretty name?

"How you doing, Mr. Pruitt?" is what she say everyday when she brings me my mail.

"Hey, baby, forget that mail and come sit with me

a little."

"Now, Mr. Pruitt, you know I can't be doing stuff like that. I got to work."

"I'll take care of you, baby. Just come on up here on the porch. You can sit on my lap if you like."

"That sounds tempting, Mr. Pruitt. And one of these days we're going to get together and do something mighty dangerous."

"We can start right now, baby."

Then we both just fall out laughing. Ain't that terrible to be teasing an old man like me? I like it though. I'm pretty much harmless. I don't think I'm dirty, just like to have my fun.

And after she gives me my mail she just switches on down the street. And the only thing you want to do is kiss God for creating the wind that blew them Kroger's advertisements out of her hands that forced her to bend over and pick up every last one of them—all sixty.

Stroke or no stroke! Lord! But I said all that to say this: Tiffany's my friend, too. Like if she don't see me on the porch by the time she brings me my mail, she'll come knocking on my door. "Mr. Pruitt, are you in there?" And if I don't answer real soon, and she know I ain't gone visiting with nobody, then nobody ain't getting a lick of mail until she finds out where her Mr. Pruitt is. Ain't that something? She even came to see me in the hospital when I had my stroke about three years ago. I told Mrs. Walters one time how nice Tiffany is.

"Umph" —this Mrs. Walters talking now —"that girl is as fast as lightning."

Mrs. Walters got her crazy ways sometimes.

"I don't see how in the world she can deliver all that mail and flirt with so many menfolks at the same time. That's something I just don't understand."

If you ask me, I think Mrs. Walters is just plain jealous of me and Tiffany. Tiffany wouldn't give one hot damn if Mrs. Walters could make it to the mailbox or not.

"And another thing, Mr. Pruitt"—Mrs. Walters getting all fired up now—"I think it's just downright sinful for her to wear them tight pants and walk around in public like that for anybody with at least one good eyeball in their socket to see." Mrs. Walters is real proper like that.

"But Mrs. Walters," I said, "I think that's a government regulated mail-carrying uniform."

"Well, Mr. Pruitt," she said, "you would think the government should also be in the business of slowing down the immorality of folks nowadays."

I don't say a word about that because it's too close to politics and there's two things I try not to discuss with folks, one is politics, the other is religion. I leave them things alone, strictly alone. Like deadly poison, I say.

As far as politics go, why discuss it? The world is going to hell in a hand-basket because of the folks we voted for or didn't vote for. I mean, Lord, what kind of fool makes promises and thinks everybody believes them? Some folks are just stupid like that. Lord! And don't that just kills you when they kiss all over babies? Fake. And what about when they make trips to some farmland to visit some poor farmer with twenty-five children and one pregnant wife, and he steps out of some beat-up truck—that ain't his, of course—wearing raggedly blue jeans, tennis shoes and some muddy baseball cap and saying something dumb like, "I understand your problems. And I know how you feel." And everybody knowing good and well that he got three bank accounts and a boat so big until you got to call it a yacht. So, what problems do he understand?

The only politician I trust will be the one that will say something like: "Y'all vote for me. I'm a liar. I'm treacherous. I'm a cheat. And to be perfectly honest with you folks, I'm just no damn good. Thank you for your support." Then he walks off the stage and don't even trying kissing on no babies because he thinks they're all filthy little puking rug rats. He don't shake nobody's hands because—let's be truthful here—he's just a little bit above us, and frankly, he really don't know where your hands been. Now, there goes an honest man. So, what's the use in discussing politics?

Same for religion. Why discuss it? Myrtle used to go to church every Sunday. Never missed a day unless she was sick. Sometimes she would make me go with her. Now, what really turned me completely off from church was that pastor of Myrtle's. I think it was Easter Sunday, or something like that. I can't remember. Anyway, we met him coming in and Myrtle said something like, "Reverend, this is my husband, Lester Pruitt. Lester, this is Reverend James Coleman."

"How you doing, James?" shaking his hand. At the same time I heard Myrtle catch her breath.

He shook my hand back, but he looked at me like I had just been christened a leper. I tell you, I couldn't have been looked at more harshly if I had passed gas right there on the front steps of St. Matthew Baptist Church.

"*Reverend* Coleman," he corrected me, smiling

that smile, like I was somebody's lost retarded child on medication.

Now, that little incident killed the day for me. Ain't that something? Him being young enough for me to be his daddy. I sat through the whole service daydreaming. I wasn't about to give this clown the benefit of me listening to his sermon. All this thinking made me remember my mother and father and my little brother, John-John, growing up in Harper. And I wonder: would my daddy get up on a cross to save some folks? Bad enough if you the guilty one; even worse if you innocent. "Who?" daddy would say, "You the one that did the crime. So your ass ought to do the time. Now hang up there and shut the hell up." And the only way I could see my daddy up there on a cross is if his mind stepped out. Then I'll have to fight and wrestle with the Romans all by myself because John-John is sitting at the foot of the cross looking up at daddy and crying and bawling and almost choking to death off his own snot and begging daddy to get down. And mama got both hands on her hips, throwing curses and threats and trying to get my daddy to come down, too.

Then somebody out in the crowd will say something stupid like: "Hey, lady, go home and take them raggedly looking children with you." And what they say that for? Now mama's picked up some stones and several big sticks and now she's whipping ass all over Calvary, chasing folks off Golgotha, and jacking up folks in their collars and letting them priests and Pharisees know they still low-class in her book and that she don't mind one bit turning Crucifixion Day completely out. Now the whole scene has changed: we all at this long dinner table eating too much fatty foods and drinking way too much wine on account there's a fellow at the table who got this trick where he can make wine out of regular tap water—but we all love each other and nobody is cussing and trying to cut anybody.

My daydreaming and sleeping probably would've gone on and on if a collection plate hadn't been shoved in my face and Myrtle poking me in the side to get me to drop something. Which I didn't, of course.

To sum the whole thing up: how many folks you know want to get crucified on account of somebody else's wrongdoings? And these somebody elses ain't even related to you on nobody's side of the family. So, you know you got to be a saint just for that alone. And instead of folks calling you Reverend Jesus, you just plain old Jesus. Ain't that something?

But I said all of that to say this: I leave religion

and politics alone. Strictly alone. And I said all that to say this: I keep quiet when Mrs. Walters is talking about those two. And I said all that to say this: she's my friend. See? I ain't lonely.

Lily Anne. She's my friend, too. But I see her only once in a blue moon. If she ain't in jail, she's down at the crazy house. Poor lost thing.

Charlie Simms stay drunker than any Baptist deacon. He's a nice man. You can usually get a good conversation out of him before he pass out. Miss Gertie. She's still my friend, too, even though she quit talking to me about a month ago when I told her that if there ever was a word for thief her grandson was it. It was no use in her getting mad. It ain't like I lied. You would think folks appreciate honesty. But she cried just the same and said she was going to miss me when she heard I was leaving Memphis.

Herman Kilinsky is an okay fellow. Sometimes. He's the fruit and vegetable man that push his cart down this street every Monday and Thursday. But some days—and I ain't shame to tell you—I want to whip this man. And it ain't cause he's white either. I got a heap of dislikings about him and we don't even have to touch that subject at all. But he's always trying to slide in some smart aleck remark about something.

Like the time that Willie boy made mayor. First black fellow to be made mayor in Memphis. So, here comes Herman pushing that raggedly cart of his one day. Matter of fact, it was the day after the election, I remember. And he smiling that smile of his. And he ask for some iced tea, so I brung him some. Both of us standing out here in the front yard just trying to admire the weather and knowing that both of us got something on our minds. He waited until he had finished the whole glass then he said, "Well, I reckon the blacks finally got what they worked hard for."

No lie, I was feeling pretty good about the outcome of the election. "Yea," I say. "I guess everything worked out just fine."

He turned the glass all the way up, his big cow tongue wiggling around the ice cubes, getting every drop of tea there was. Finally, he burps: a deep nastily old burp. Then he say, "Well, I guess us white folks best leave Memphis." Then he laugh his laugh like it was the funniest thing the both of us ever heard.

Except I ain't laughing; I'm hot. "Then take your redneck ass on then. And you can just haul anybody else that favors with you!" I even stamped my feet to let him know that I meant business.

But he steady laughing at me.

"Ha! Ha! Mr. Pruitt!"

"A ha-ha hell!"

"All now, Mr. Pruitt. No use you getting all tight-jawed. Just a little joke. Don't mean nothing by that. Easy now."

"Well, you just watch what you say. Don't have me whip your ass."

He fell out laughing again, almost crying. "Mr. Pruitt, you something else! I declare, you something else! A sight!" He can't wipe the tears quick enough. "Well, I best get along, Mr. Pruitt. I sure don't want you whipping all over me and I still got almost a whole day's work ahead of me."

"You best get along," I tell him.

Him steady laughing at me cause he really can't see a sixty year old man getting whipped by a seventy-five year old man with a partially paralyzed left side. But I swear, I would've tried if he said another word. One mumbling word.

But instead, he gave me my glass back, still laughing, and started pushing that raggedly fruit cart of his down the street like he's some big-shot corporate president and that damn cart of his is his Mercedes-Benz. Ain't that something? I think if you plan to look down on folks, you ought to stand on something high enough. How in the hell can you look down when you wallowing in a ditch yourself?

Just look at him. Kilinsky been hollering, Apples! Peaches! Collards and carrots, since the fifties. And this ain't no side job either; so don't let him tell you different.

But I said all that to say this: Herman Kilinsky ain't my everyday friend like them other folks I mentioned. He's an every-once-in-a-while kind of friend. We could be real good friends if I never see him. He came by yesterday to say good-bye. Thank God that's the last time I'll see him and that damn cart of his.

Now, in case you wondering why I decided to leave Memphis all of a sudden, I'll tell you. I ran into a heap of money. And when I say heap, I mean HEAP.

It all started about three months ago. It was raining something awful one day, and Lord, it would be my grocery day. So, I put on me some clothes, got my umbrella and even put on some old hat. No use in catching pneumonia.

I didn't get no farther than the steps in front of my house when I fell. It was my stroke side, too. Didn't know one bit that I had fractured my hipbone. I just picked myself up and went on because I love me some grocery shopping and I'll walk through hell and the northern part of Georgia in order to make my grocery shopping day. I am a fool for good eating, and I don't care who knows it. Anyway, I don't miss my grocery day is what I'm trying to relate to you.

The accident happened on aisle nine, which, of course, now is my favorite number (never mind what store it was, cause part of the agreement was to keep my mouth shut).

I was almost through with my shopping, and the last thing I had to get was my coffee. The only thing I love more than eating is drinking my coffee. I love me some coffee. And I don't mean that nasty flavored coffee, either. I'm a Maxwell House fool from way back. I love to sip on my coffee while watching my favorite show. And that's *Jerry Springer*. I love my *Jerry Springer*. If you a big enough fool to air your dirty laundry on national television for the whole world to see, then I have no problem in pouring myself a cup of Maxwell House and watching. Can't nobody lead a bigger parade of white trash like that Jerry Springer can. I swear!

Anyway, I stroll—the best way I know how since my hip was beginning to pain me a little—on over to aisle nine to get my coffee. I even had a fifty-cent off coupon, too, so you know I was ready, as the saying goes. Down that aisle is where I slipped. Lost my balance in a puddle of apple juice. Actually, I didn't even hit the ground, cause I caught hold of my shopping basket just in time. I couldn't believe it: two accidents in one day. I hurt my pinky finger this time.

And right when I'm trying to haul myself up, this fellow walks by, who I find out later was the manager and he had not too long ago told one of the stock boys to mop up the juice. When he saw me he screamed.

"Mister, you okay?"

"Just fine. Help me up, will ya?"

"No. I want you to lie down. Here, I help you.

"No, fellow, I'm okay. Just let me be."

But he already had me down on the floor, stretched out, so I really couldn't do nothing but keep quiet and enjoy the scenery—the scenery being every customer in the whole damn store hauling it over to aisle number nine to catch a peek at the floor show I was putting on.

"Now just stay there, Mister. I'm going to call an ambulance for you."

"But I—"

"No, Mister!"

So I shut up.

Do I need to say more? I mean, do I have to mention I was taken to Baptist Hospital? A 'routine' X-ray showed I had a fractured hipbone? Do I have to mention my niece, Rose, almost had kittens when she found out her Uncle Lester was sick? And was threatening to sue the whole city of Memphis? Do I have to mention I was in the hospital again—the first time was when I had my stroke about three years ago—for about two months? And do I have to tell you that one day while I was in the hospital two fellows come up to my room and told me that they represented So and So Grocery Stores and they are willing to pay me about a pile of money so high and all I have to do is sign these papers that basically said that I forgive them and I won't sic my niece on them? Need I mention that I signed and took the check and hid it under my bed and not a soul know a thing? Not even Rose?

Need I mention the first thing I did when I got out of the hospital was to cash the check, put the money in a grocery sack, put the house up for sell? And I'm planning to go live with my niece, Rose, and her husband and Eddie, Jr. just as soon as she get here. Do I need to mention this?

You know, I think I'll give some of this money to

Eddie, Jr. He's planning to go to the University of Memphis this year. I wish you could see him. That fellow sure has grown. Looking just like his daddy. Poor thing. Rose and Big Eddie always wanted one of them big dens in the back of the house with a pool table and one of them big TV's and a tank full of them fishes with the big eyeballs. I think that will be nice, just nice.

So, I'm bound for the Promised Land. But it sure ain't in the hell Canaan. I'm going to Olive Branch, Mississippi. That's where my niece, Rose, live. She'll be here in a few minutes to get me and take me away from here. I going to miss this place. Not going to lie about that. You just can't pick up and leave a place after plenty of years and not miss it. You just can't.

You know, I might even buy her a car, since the one she been driving she been driving a long time. I think she will like that.

The Presence of Angels

A sharp breeze swayed the stiff tulips that stood around the edges of the grave. They were plastic tulips, but they were just as pretty.

Every month or so, a new batch of plastic flowers—not always tulips though—were planted around the grave of Mr. Elliot James. He died of a heart attack six years ago.

Millie, his wife, planted these flowers. Usually on the first Sunday, she came out here with a light lunch of ham and cheese and milk, or a small Thermos of soup, along with a tiny stool that she had bought from a Salvation Army store, and sat with her husband. Sometimes she brought her bible out here to the grave—just in case the conversation got too boring.

She loved talking to Mr. James. She told him that their daughter had just graduated from Memphis State. She told him about the time she, Millie, had slipped in a pothole in the driveway and scarred her knee—her left knee. She told him when the Johnsons, their neighbors, had bought a new car and were getting ready to take a trip to California to see their son who had just passed the bar. She told him about the time she was almost mugged in the parking lot of Lord and Taylor's. She retold the story that she had heard from a lady she met in Kroger whose brother's oldest son's best friend was arrested for murder. She told him that Nora Mae, the housekeeper, just had another baby—her third. She told him that a new street was being built between Poplar and Central, a couple of blocks away from their home. She told him that she had found a little puppy in her neighborhood and decided to keep it. When Millie had finally told Mr. James everything that she could think of, she opened up her brown paper bag and started on her lunch.

One Sunday Millie was sitting at the grave crying, even though this was a nice crisp February afternoon.

"Elliot, I'm scared." She wiped the tears that were quickly forming. "I got to have an operation. Gall stones. Dr. Poole said I got gall stones bigger than melons." She blew her nose and sniffed. "Well, he didn't exactly say as big as melons. But he did say they were big. Lord, Elliot, I'm scared. Suppose I die? I'm not that scared to die. I believe when you got to go, you got to go. But I sure would hate to go in a gall stone operation. I always see myself going in a real nice way. I mean, like running into the street and saving some child who's about to be hit by a car. Now, that's a nice way to go." She dried her eyes again. "But, Elliot, don't get me wrong. Heart attacks are a proud way to go, but it's not for me." She looked down at the handkerchief that she had been twisting and pulling ever since she had been out here. "Too bad we don't have a choice on how to leave." She ate her sandwich of ham and cheese, then, packing up everything, including her little stool, said good-bye to Mr. James and sullenly left the cemetery.

~~~~~

Three months passed. It was an April, another Sunday afternoon when Millie came back with a new batch of plastic flowers. She was much thinner now, healthier. She even had a permanent in her hair, and the grey around her temples gave her that sophisticated middle-aged look.

"I'm back, Elliot," she said to the grave, smiling, situating herself: sitting on her stool, setting her purse and lunch bag down, and then, finally, her bible. "Thought sure I would be good as dead by now." She laughed for thinking such a silly thought.

"But here I am. The operation was a success. Them folks were so nice. Can't say too much for the food, but the folks were nice. Elliot, I met the cutest little thing in the hospital. She was my nurse. Came in every day just a-smiling and giving shots. She was so cute. Wasn't no taller than that needle she was toting. Wasn't nothing but twenty-three years old. Just got out of school. When I first saw her walking in my room with that needle I said, 'Honey, you sure you know how to work that thing?' and she just smiled and said, 'I sure do, Mrs. James,' and she did too, Elliot. Worked that thing right in my cheek." She laughed some more. "Cutest little thing you ever wanted to see."

She stopped talking for a moment to get her ham and cheese sandwich out of the sack. "They let me have my stones. I got them in my purse right now. I don't know what I'm going to do with them. Nora Mae told me when her daddy came out of the hospital—he had the same operation you know—he had his stones set in a pair of diamond earrings for her mama for her birthday. Now that's lovely." She had already finished her sandwich and was now sipping on a carton of low-fat milk.

It was at that moment when she noticed a freshly packed grave about two rows over from Mr. James.

"Oh, Elliot, I believe you got a new neighbor. Please excuse me." She stood up, wiping bread crumbs from the dress Nora Mae had suggested she wear, and quickly walked over to the fresh grave. She stood at the foot and studied the tombstone. After awhile she came back to her stool. "I declare, Elliot. That poor child. Wasn't nothing but twenty-five years old. Born April seventeenth and died on his birthday. Wow. He was a Conway. Didn't we know some Conways back in Harper? Can't think of their names right now, but we knew some. I bet his folks are just torn up. Somebody that young." She shook her head. "A pity." She packed up everything, said good-bye to Mr. James, and sullenly left the cemetery.

~~~~~

The next month was the month Millie noticeed a young woman at the grave of the young man who had died on his birthday. Millie was reading her bible, the Creation being her favorite story, when she first saw her. Of course, she stopped reading. "That must be his girlfriend," she whispered to Mr. James. "I definitely don't see a ring. At least not from here." She immediately stood up, grabbed her purse, and started walking toward the girl.

The girl was sitting on the ground, Indian-style,

stripping a blade of grass. She was looking blankly into the grave, and her back was toward Millie, so she didn't see or hear her approaching.

"Hello, how are you?"

The girl looked up. "Fine." The girl had been crying, and now, her eyes were red and her whole face was puffy. She looked back at the grave.

"Was this your husband?" Millie suddenly noticed how young this girl was. She even reminded Millie of her daughter.

"No."

"Your boyfriend?"

"Woman, can't you leave me alone? Can't a person sit in a cemetery and be depressed in peace? Leave me alone!"

"Well, honey, I didn't mean to—"

"Just go!"

Millie wanted to cry. She wasn't used to being talked to like this. She quickly walked back to her stool. "Elliot, that child's meaner than a cut ape. Almost ate me alive." She clenched the collar of her dress as though she had just narrowly escaped some horrid accident. "You know, I thought she looked like Maggie, but I know she couldn't be our daughter. Maggie wouldn't dare be so mean." She glanced at the girl, then she opened her bible and began reading again.

This was a nice day. A pretty postcard day: the grass in the cemetery was a nice deep green, the flowers— red, yellow, pink—perfect. This was one of the reasons why Millie visited the cemetery. Millie loved beautiful things. Even on her fingers she had two beautiful rings: a huge diamond and a sparkling ruby. Around her neck: pearls.

Suddenly, Millie realized a horrible thought: "Elliot, I think I might have been a little bit nosey. You think so? It wasn't none of my business who that child was. I think I'll go apologize to that sweet girl."

But the girl must have sensed Millie's intentions, for, she—the girl—turned and glared at Millie, and Millie, who had already stood, caught the look and slowly sat back down.

"Lord, Elliot," Millie said, "she's meaner than a yard dog." Millie watched her from a distance, flickering her eyes from her bible to the girl, then back again.

Later, about early evening, Millie packed up everything and left. The girl was still sitting Indian-style at the grave.

Several months had passed and Millie had only visited Mr. James twice since her encounter with the girl. Millie had been busy. Her daughter, Maggie, was getting married. The Rotary Club was raising money to buy a new fountain. Nora Mae's oldest child had the flu, so Millie had to clean the house herself. Millie's Aunt Linnie came to visit the last part of June. She saw a woman crying on Union Avenue, and after stopping to find out what was wrong, had spent the last three weeks helping this woman hide from an abusive husband. She had a birthday during the last week in July—fifty-four. She accidentally slipped again in that pothole in her driveway. She got a new car—a Lincoln. She got the pothole in the driveway fixed—eighty-five dollars.

So, when Millie finally made it back to Forrest Hill Cemetery, she had a lot to tell him. She was talking to Mr. James for almost an hour when she suddenly saw a shadow come across his grave. She quickly turned around to see the girl—the girl that yelled at her the last time she was here.

"Hello," Millie smiled, but a nervous smile because she wasn't too sure about this girl.

"Hello," the girl said back, but quite bleakly. She stared at Millie for a couple of seconds.

Millie stared back, waiting for something to happen.

"I'm sorry. I didn't mean it. I been hoping to see

you again to tell you that I was sorry."

"No, honey," said Millie, feeling a little relief now. "Don't you apologize to me. I should be apologizing to you. What I asked you wasn't none of my business. You did right by telling me to go away. I don't know who I thought I was. You done right, because if I were you I would've said the same thing to me. So, honey, please forgive me."

The girl smiled. "Okay. You're forgiven."

Millie smiled back.

"He was my brother."

"Who?"

The girl nodded her head toward the other grave that now looked almost like the others.

"Oh." That was all Millie had said. She watched the girl, who was now looking down at her skirt, slowly tracing the outline of a flower with her index finger. It was obvious to Millie that the girl wanted to talk. "So, what's your name?"

"Maggie."

Mille almost fell over backwards trying to get up off the stool. "Really?"

Maggie looked at Mille like she had a hole in her head. "Yeah. That's the name my mama gave me."

"Lord, what a coincidence. My daughter's name is Maggie. She's getting married, you know. Marrying

161

a doctor."

"Really?" Actually, Maggie didn't care.

"She hadn't too long graduated from Memphis State."

"Really?"

"Yeah. Now she's marrying a doctor. Time can surely get away from you if you're not careful."

"Really?"

"Yeah, I was just telling Nora Mae the same exact thing."

"Who's Nora Mae?"

"My housekeeper. She just had a baby, you know. The cutest little thing you ever wanted to see."

"Really?"

Millie finally realized that Maggie didn't care. "My name's Millie." The girl made no reaction. Millie looked around a moment and then: "I got an extra sandwich of ham and cheese, and I'm about to eat lunch. Would you please join me?"

Maggie thought about it, then she sat down, facing Millie. "Thank you," she finally said.

Millie smiled.

For the next several months, off and on, Millie and Maggie met at the cemetery and had a light lunch together. Millie still didn't know a thing about Maggie. The girl simply did not talk much.

But that was okay. Millie did most, if not all, of the talking. Millie enjoyed Maggie's company.

One afternoon, however, when Millie was giving details about the succulent rump roast Nora Mae had cooked the day before, Maggie blurted out: "I used to be married."

This caught Millie off guard. Surprisingly, she was speechless. She wanted to ask a question but she was afraid the girl might quit talking.

"—but he's not around anymore. He was sleeping with the neighborhood 'ho'. That's when I was waitressing at Zinnie's. I came home early one day and before I could get through the front door good I heard all of this moaning and bumping and carrying on in the back bedroom."

Millie blushed and grabbed the collar of her blouse, something that she did whenever she was nervous or uneasy; the subject of sex or any type of lewdness definitely made her uncomfortable. But this story was interesting, so she leaned slightly forward on her stool to make sure that she didn't miss one word.

"—so I tip-toed on into the bedroom and there they were! As naked as jaybirds!"

"Maggie, no!"

"Yes. Naked on the new bed sheets I got from K-

Mart!"

"So, what did you say?"

"I didn't say a word. I let Mr. Charlie do the talking."

"Who's Mr. Charlie?"

"My pistol."

Millie snatched at her collar: "My God, you shot him!"

"No, I didn't. But don't you think I wouldn't had. All I needed for him to say was just one word. One damn word and I would've cleaned all fifteen teeth out of his head! That's how mad I was."

Millie saw that Maggie was enjoying telling this story. "So, what did the girl say?"

"What you think she said? Not a damn word. Anyway, she was too busy crawling out the window."

"In the nude?"

"Naked."

"My Lord."

"Then he come saying to me 'baby, I love you' and 'baby, I didn't mean for this to happen' and 'baby, you know you're the only one' and baby this and baby that. And I said to him, 'Nigger, if you baby me one more time, I'm going to put so many holes in your ass until you going to look like a damn sponge!' And he got quiet, too."

Millie burst into laughter, almost falling off her stool. She laughed until tears ran down her face. Maggie was laughing, also, but not as hard as Millie.

Though this Sunday was another bright sunny day, the cemetery was almost empty—except for a graveside funeral—but that was taking place way across on the other side of the park, so the mourners couldn't hear these two women screaming with laughter.

They were still laughing when they packed up, waved good-bye, and went their separate ways— Millie already excited about meeting Maggie again.

But the next time Millie saw Maggie at the cemetery, Maggie wasn't speaking. She was sitting Indian-style at the grave of her brother. Millie left her alone.

~~~~~

The next month, Millie was carrying on a heated debate with Mr. Elliot about the Ford trial when Maggie came up and said hello. Millie quickly said hello back, but she had to finish this argument with Mr. Elliot.

Maggie walked over to her brother's grave and sat down.

By now, Millie was just flat out disgusted over Mr. Elliot's views. She promptly got up, vowed never to speak to him again, and went over to where Maggie was sitting.

Immediately, Maggie asked, "Why do you talk to that mound of dirt like that?"

Millie thought for a moment, then: "I know Elliot isn't really there. Elliot's everywhere I am and I know he watches me. We had been married almost over twenty years and we got to knowing each other pretty well all those years. We knew what the other was thinking long before we could get the words out of our mouths. So, it's all right for me to talk to that mound of dirt like that. I know Elliot is probably an angel somewhere, but often I can actually feel his presence. I slipped in a pothole a couple of months ago. I know Elliot saw it and he felt bad for me. When my daughter announced that she was getting married, I know me and Elliot rejoiced at the same time."

Almost a whole minute had passed before she spoke again, and when she did, she had a slight look of horror. "But I wonder—", she looked directly at Maggie, "I wonder do the dead look at us in a pitiful grieving way, like they see us quickly heading for some profound tragedy and they can't tell us that we had better slow down. What do you think?"

Maggie had a small smirk on her face. "I think you're crazier than a damn road lizard. That's what I think."

Millie burst into tears. "You're the most evil child I ever laid eyes on." She got up, grabbed her stool, and went back to Mr. James' grave. "Elliot, she's the most evil child I ever laid eyes on." She sat with her back toward Maggie and wept silently.

Maggie repented. She got up from the ground and went over to where Mille was sitting. "I'm sorry," she said to Millie's back. She walked around to face her, but Millie turned on her stool. Maggie tried facing her again, but Millie turned. "I'm sorry." Maggie was really sorry this time. She sat down behind Mille and began stripping a blade of grass, a habit that she had now since coming to this cemetery.

An hour had passed and still they both sat. Millie had stopped crying, and she was now looking across the quiet cemetery—looking at nothing in particular. More like in a daze, Maggie steady stripping blades of grass. And they sat.

"My brother killed himself," Maggie started off. "One day—his birthday, in fact—he just blew his head off."

Suddenly, this nice sunny Sunday was turning

cloudy: thick rain clouds, like dirty cotton balls, were forming in the skies. Both women took notice of this, but neither said anything about it.

"He once told me that he had no friends. I told him to quit talking like that cause he got friends. Plenty of friends. But he tells me all his friends just know his first and last name and nothing more. I kept telling him to stop talking like that, but at the same time I saw him slowly slip away and I didn't do a thing." She was getting teary eyed.

A light drizzle had started, but still the women sat.

"Mama and daddy raised us differently. My brother was brought up by two stupid teenagers who didn't know a damn thing about raising a child. By the time they realized their mistake, my brother was already lost. They tried making it up by the time I came along." Another tear had fallen. "My brother was emotionally disturbed. In and out of the hospital, and between that he stayed drunk. I feel guilty about that." She wiped her face. "I know I wasn't the cause of his death, but sometimes I say to myself, 'why couldn't it be me and not him?' If I could, I would've traded ten years of my life for one minute of peace for my brother. Instead, I slowly watched him slip away into nothing. The last thing he said to me was that this world wasn't made to accommodate lonely people."

The rain picked up and Maggie was crying. Both women didn't seem to notice the rain. Without speaking, Maggie got up and left. Millie started to say something to her, but instead, she said to Mr. James, "Elliot, now there goes a troubled soul."

Winter came and went and Millie hadn't seen Maggie. But one early spring Sunday Millie saw Maggie sitting at her brother's grave.

Before Maggie could speak, Maggie asked, "Do you think I'm crazy?"

Somehow, Millie wasn't surprised by this question. Even though it had been almost a year and she still didn't know this girl, Millie knew her enough to know that this girl was hard to know. "No, I don't think you're crazy."

"Well, I think you are."

This didn't surprise Millie either. She laughed at herself for being so clever.

"In fact, you're the craziest white woman I've seen in a long time."

Millie fell out laughing.

Maggie reached down into the front of her dress, her bra, and pulled out a small joint.

Millie grabbed her collar. "What's that?"

"Peace." She lit it and smoked.

"Honey, isn't that illegal?"

"If you get caught it sure in the hell is." She offered it to Millie, but she only flapped it away. "Suit yourself. Say, tell me about your husband."

"What about him?"

"Anything."

"Well, I loved him. Still do. Provided for his family quite well, even after his death. He was a lawyer. Had his own practice. He was a good man. Maggie loved him." She paused for a moment as though she wanted to go on but couldn't.

Maggie sensed this.

"—but it was so hard for him to show any feelings. You know, no kissing, touching, nothing. Everything was business to him. Business. Even our decision to have our daughter was like a business deal."

"Have you ever had an affair?"

Now, this shocked Millie. Blushing, then playing with her collar: "Well, sort of."

Maggie clapped her hands in triumph. "I knew you were faking this Miss Goody-Two-Shoes look. Who was it?"

Millie darted her head from side to side to make sure no one was around. As usual, there was no one in the cemetery. But she leaned forward and whispered anyway. "The man who came to install our satellite television."

"No."

"Yes." She looked over at her husband's grave, then she whispered, "Of course, we didn't do anything. We almost did, but then the satellite dish fell over in the backyard and created this huge noise and I knew it was a sign from God. That stopped us both in our tracks."

Maggie laughed.

"Of course, Elliot never found out. I thought he did, because when we got the bill the man had charged us a hundred dollars less than the actual cost and Elliot commented on how generous the man was and I almost dropped the plate of chicken I was bringing into the dining room at that time."

Maggie laughed.

"Lord, that scared me. I was nervous for a good two whole months. I couldn't sleep. I looked awful—like two burned holes in a bedspread. Didn't tell anybody. Not even Nora Mae, and I tell her everything." She frowned to herself, "I think it was all Elliot's fault. If he would've"—she was trying to think of a delicate way to put it—"done his duty as a man, I wouldn't have been looking anywhere else.

Everything was business to him. Business."

Maggie offered her the joint again. Millie hesitated at first, commented that she couldn't believe that she was about to smoke some pot, then she took it and put it up to her mouth. Maggie had to tell her what to do. Her first puff, she gagged. By the fifth hit, she was smiling.

After it was gone, Maggie pulled out another joint from her bra.

"I declare," Millie said, "how many of them things you got up there?"

"Let me put it this way," Maggie said, "these breasts cost me a good two hundred dollars."

They both fell out laughing. An hour later: stoned.

Millie stared at Maggie's brother's tombstone. "THE LORD GIVETH, AND THE LORD TAKETH AWAY" Millie thought for a moment. "Hey, you know what my tombstone is going to say?"

"What?" Maggie asked.

"SEE? I TOLD YOU I WASN'T FEELING WELL."

They laughed.

Maggie said, "Mine might say: 'I CRIED A LITTLE, LAUGHED A LITTLE, AND DIED A WHOLE LOT' If you ask me, that's the summation of everybody's life."

They held their heads in reverence.

"Nora Mae said her tombstone is going to say: 'I ATE AT NEWBY'S'"

They laughed.

"I really don't believe that this Nora Mae person exists. Nora Mae this and Nora Mae that."

"She is a real person."

The women began to argue over the existence of Nora Mae. This lasted about five minutes.

"She's at my house right now."

"Let's go see her then."

"Okay."

It took them longer than usual to pack up. Millie still had a joint in her hand, and she looked around to figure out where she ought to put it. A twinkle jumped in her eyes. She walked over to Mr. James' grave and dug a tiny hole. "Here, Elliot," she said, "pucker up." She planted the joint on the grave.

Maggie applauded.

~~~~~

Millie started the car and tried following the black winding road that slithered through the cemetery like a snake. Instantly, she drove off the path and smacked the new Lincoln into a tombstone. They both laughed. Millie shifted into reverse, but only to drive across the path and into another tombstone. They howled! It was a good ten minutes before they could stop laughing.

Suddenly, Maggie stopped laughing. "Do you think we could be friends forever and ever?"

Millie thought about this question for moment. "I don't know, honey. I suppose we could. I don't have anything else planned." Millie thought some more, and this answer seemed to satisfy the both of them.

She started driving again—slowly. She followed the path through the cemetery. When she got to the end, she looked both ways, then slowly pulled out into the busy street.

A Trip to the Fair

I see on TV that the fair is coming to town. I ask Mama if we going and she say yeah. Then I ask her can I ride the Ferris wheel and eat some corn dogs and see the fat lady. Mama say quit asking so many questions 'cause she got work to do. But I steady keep asking until she say: "Sonny Buck, quit worrying your poor Mama."

I quit asking, but I'm so excited until I can't sit still. Even when *The Dukes of Hazard* and the Evel Knievel special come on where he's gonna jump over twenty cars and through a ring of fire, I still got the Mid-South Fair in the back of my head. I can't shake it. Even when I'm sleeping I can't dream of nothing but going to the fair and riding the Ferris wheel and eating food. I even wake up in the middle of the night out of breath from riding a ride too much. I even wake one day thinking it is Saturday when it is only Friday and there is no going to the fair yet.

So finally Saturday get here and I'm sitting outside on the curb talking to Kicky and his sister

Monica, who are sitting on the other side of the street on account they excited too about getting to the fair and we talking about what all we gonna do this year, what we did last year, and what other folks on our block did at the fair. So they ain't been sleeping good either. They eating peanut butter-and-jelly sandwiches.

"Oh, I can't wait. I want to ride The Pippin!" say Kicky. His eyes getting big just by telling the story, licking the sticky jelly that's creeping down his arms.

"I ain't getting on that damn thing!" say Monica. I can see her getting all nervous from across the street, but steady munching on her sandwich.

They are always cussing and carrying on. Mama say they are bad and half-raised, and their mama is a bum. "They the cussingest little children you ever wanna come across!" say Mama.

"What you gonna ride, Sonny Buck?"

"I don't know," I say. "I mean, I do know, but I don't know the name of it. The Spider thing."

Monica get excited. "Oh! I love me that!"

We stay outside and talk for a long time. Sometimes other folks—Barry, Wayne, Boo or anybody else whose mama and daddy let them cross the streets—come riding by on their bikes or skates or just walking, and they telling us what they riding or what prize they gonna try and win.

Pretty soon when it's getting almost dark everybody go in the house that is going to the fair with their mamas and daddys. In fact, nobody got to be called inside tonight.

~~~~~

We at Big Ma's house. She live down the street from us. We stop by before going to the fair. She look sad, all frowning up and stuff, but I pay this no never mind cause Big Ma is always frowning up about something. Mama said she got bad nerves.

I tell Big Ma that we going to the fair. She pat me on the head and say, "That's nice, baby." I ask Big Ma if she got cake. She always do—in the kitchen wrapped in foil on the table. She said she already cut me a piece and told me to go get it. When I go to the kitchen I hear her fussing at Daddy and Mama. Telling them they ought to be ashamed of they selves. And Mama saying back, "Just for a couple of hours, Mama. You know how he is always falling asleep."

I eat my cake in the kitchen cause for some reason—I don't know why—I figured they talking about me some kind of way. Even when I'm done eating my cake I stay put in the kitchen cause I feel like something ain't what it supposed to be. But then I hear Big Ma holler and ask me what I'm doing back there, so I come on out and they looking at me: Mama and Daddy looking at me. Big Ma looking at me. Daddy looking wild—looking like he want to start laughing, but thinking he better not. Mama keep darting her eyes at me, then at Big Ma, then at Daddy, and back at me again. Then when I look at Big Ma she look sad at me.

Mama was the first person to say something. "Say, Sonny Buck. What Big Ma got for you in her bedroom?"

"I don't know."

"You better go see. It might need feeding."

The first thing I'm thinking is that Big Ma got me a dog or a lizard or something else to play with cause she say one day she is going to get me a pet. So I forget about them and run in Big Ma bedroom that's all the way in the back of the house. The room is dark and cold so I turn on the light. Nothing. I don't see nothing.

"Where that dog at, Big Ma?"

She say nothing.

I run back up front to ask her again cause I'm figuring she didn't hear me the first time. But there ain't nobody here in the living room. I see Big Ma standing out on the porch fussing. I don't see Mama or Daddy at all. I run out on the porch with her and as soon as I see them in the car I start hollering and screaming and crying on account they trick me again about taking me somewhere and leaving me here with Big Ma.

I see Mama's head leaning over out the car. "Sonny Buck, stay there with Big Ma. We gonna be right back."

"But I want to go to the fair too!"

"Fair? What fair? We ain't going to no fair. What's makes you think we going to some fair?"

I can't answer. I don't know why I think that.

"We ain't going to no fair," Mama say again.

I start crying even louder and start rubbing my fists in my eyes.

Big Ma patting me on the shoulder to calm me down, but there ain't no calming down when folks are going to the fair and you can't go. So I get louder with each pat she give me.

Finally, Daddy say, "All right, send him on."

Before Big Ma can say go get my coat, I already run in the house and grabbed my coat.

I jump in the back seat and I can't stop grinning. I look out the window at Big Ma.

She smiling at me. I wave at her. She wave back.

~~~~~

Now we in the car—we being me, Mama and Daddy—and we can't sit still for two seconds. Even though Daddy and especially Mama pretend like it ain't nothing, but they excited too.

"Don't nothing draw a bigger crowd of white trash like a state fair," Mama is always saying. Then she get to shaking her head like it's a pure tragedy. But she just as excited as anybody else in the car. She like those big smoked turkey legs as big as your thighs, the kind that squirt turkey juice everywhere when you bite one.

Daddy like looking at the fights in the parking lot and the freaky people in the tents. He is always falling out laughing when he see the fights or the freaks.

So we get to the fair and there's lights and lights and noise and more lights and people screaming and laughing and all kinds of happenings going on. In fact, so much is happening I get dizzy trying to look at all of it. I start breathing hard.

"Calm down, Sonny Buck," say Mama.

The first thing we do is get Mama's turkey leg. She munching and pointing and saying how good her turkey is. She lean down and give me a bite. It is good and I ask for another. Then another, until finally Mama said: "Look, Sonny Buck." Which is the same as saying: Now, you ain't gonna eat all of my leg!

So we walking all through the fair looking at folks and smelling the foods. I'm walking between Mama and Daddy and they both holding my hands.

Then Daddy see the tent where the freak people are and he ask Mama if she want to go in there with him.

"I don't think so!" say Mama, steady munching on her turkey leg even though we got that when we first got here.

"Well, I think I'm going in."

"I wanna go, Daddy!" I say.

"Well, come on," he say.

"Well, I'm going too," say Mama. "Hard enough as it is to keep up with you two menfolks."

So the three of us march in and the first thing we see is the fat lady. She's sitting down watching TV. *Starsky and Hutch* is on. She act like she don't see us, even though there's a bunch of us looking at her.

Daddy laughing at hisself.

Mama shaking her head like it's a shame.

"How much you weigh?"

Mama slap me on the back of my head, and all the other folks standing in the tent with us just fall out laughing.

The fat lady don't even turn around but keep watching the TV like she don't hear what I just ask her.

I stare at her. Mama is always saying it ain't right to stare, but we all doing it. But she never turn around. Just steady watch TV.

We move on down and see a man with big feet. I look at him a little bit. Not much cause he's drinking beer and cussing and laughing with the folks who come to see him and his feet. Mama make me go on down to the next booth.

Daddy stay with the man with the big feet.

In the next booth the speaker is yacking about seeing the Siamese twins. I tell Mama I don't want to see no cats. She ask me what I'm talking about.

"Cats," I say. "What's so special about some cats?" But when I look over in the booth I don't see no cats. I see two men. Well, one man. No, two men. I don't know. They look alike and they sitting real close to each other, but they only got one leg apiece, but they got two legs together. I grab Mama hands because I ain't too sure about what is happening.

I look at them. They are sitting on a funny made chair watching *Starsky and Hutch*, too. I wonder do he know.....they know that the fat lady is watching the same show. I keep looking at them.

Finally, I got to say something to see if they....he can talk. I am standing at the edge of the booth. I raise my hands and wave. "Hello," I say.

One of the heads keeps watching TV. The other one turn to me and wave back. "Hello," it said back.

Now I am happy. They...it spoke to me. I look up at Mama. She looking nervous like she ready to go but she don't say nothing.

I look at them some more. They steady watching TV.

"I'm seven years old."

Both heads turned to look at me. "You are?" one of them said. "You're a big boy, aren't you?"

"Uh-huh," I say back.

Both heads smiling at me.

I look up at Mama. She looking like she want to be home with her turkey leg.

I stick my hand over the booth cause I want them to touch me. Shake my hand. Mama lean over and slap my hand back.

They smile.

By this time some giggling white woman and drunk man come walking up through the crowd and they standing almost right next to me and

Mama. And they smell like all kinds of alcohols. They can't stop giggling and howling. Everybody else is looking at them, too.

"Say, can I have a picture with you guys?"

The Siamese turn and look at the drunk man. "Yeah," the Siamese said.

He try to be cool and jump over the counter of the booth like they do on those kung fu movies or something, but instead he trip and fall and bang his head against a table that's in the booth with the Siamese.

The giggling white woman get all down in the ground she laughing so hard now. I can't stop looking at her. I look up at Mama and she still shaking her head like she can't believe what she seeing. The drunk man pop up like he meant to do that and stick his head between the Siamese heads.

I don't see nobody else except the drunk man and the giggling lady. I can't stop looking at them. She steady snapping pictures and giggling. The drunk man keep posing with the Siamese.

I keep staring at her. Finally, she stop snapping the camera and turn and look at me. She look at me like she want to smack me or something. She look like she was about to say something to me, but then she look above my head and see Mama standing there.

The woman don't say nothing but try to help the drunk man crawl back over to the other side with us. She staring at me all the time, and I'm looking back at her. She ain't giggling no more, but looking at me like I cussed at her or something. The drunk man laughing and talking out loud and calling the Siamese "dudes" and "my good friends" and trying to get the not-giggling lady started up again. But she ain't laugh ever since she saw me see her.

Then they suddenly disappear as fast as they got here. I look at Mama and she just shake her head.

I look over at the Siamese and the head that spoke to me the first time just smile and hunch up his shoulders at me like he don't know what that was all about.

I smile back cause it made me laugh, too.

Mama steady shake her head like she just can't believe none of this.

"You ready to go, Sonny Buck?"

I look over at the Siamese. I want to hang out with them some more.

"Hey," I say. "How do y'all use the bathroom?"

The next thing I know Mama snatch me and we walking out of the tent. I turn around and the Siamese are laughing and slapping each other on the back. They wave at me, and they are smiling.

I wave back at them. I wanted to say something else—I don't know what—but something. But Mama already marching me out of the tent.

"Lord Jesus child. I can't take you nowhere can I?" She looking like she want to slap my face.

I just look at her cause I ain't too sure what she talking about. She looking down at me all frown up just like Big Ma. I drop my head cause I'm shame.

She look at me a long time. I don't see her looking at me, but I feel it. First she start sniggling. Then she start laughing. First it was soft laughing, like when you don't want nobody to know you laughing. Then all of a sudden she laughing out loud and she can't stop. She look like she might be crying she laughing so hard.

"I can't believe you ask them how they use the bathroom!" She can't stop laughing. "Boy, where do you come up with all this mess?" She wiping her face. Folks are looking at Mama like she crazy or something, but she steady laughing. "Sonny Buck, I'm going to slap your face if you ever ask anybody else again." But she almost on the ground she laughing so hard.

Pretty soon Daddy catch up with us and is about to tell us what the big feet man said, but when he see Mama he start laughing and want to know what's so funny.

"I'll tell you later," trying to catch her breath. "But this boy of yours is going to put me in an early grave!" And she don't stop laughing.

Daddy pat me on the head.

~~~~~

Later on the three of us are on the Ferris wheel and we're going round and round and round. I am sitting between Mama and Daddy. I like looking out across the way and seeing all the people and the lights. Last time I was on the Ferris wheel with them I fall asleep and I had to make up stories about what I did at the fair to Kicky and Monica. I tell myself I ain't going to do that this time. We go round and round some more and I am so happy until Mama got to tap my legs to make me sit still.

I close my eyes. When I open them again I hear Daddy telling me to keep still. He is trying to take off my shoes. I'm not sure when I got home, but when Daddy pull the covers up, I grab them, ball myself up and go back to sleep.

Printed in the United States
35893LVS00001BA/169-240